Three Women

LUCY TERTIA GEORGE grew up in a theatrical family. She performs as a singer and stand-up comedian under the name Lucy Lyrical. She lives in London with her two sons and runs her own public relations agency. This is her first novel.

The cover incorporates an image entitled 'New York, New York. Italian-Americans relaxing on Sunday, 1942', taken by Marjory Collins and courtesy of the Library of Congress Prints and Photographs Division. The background fabric is from a photo by John Mallinson.

Lucy Tertia George

Three Women

by

Lucy Tertia George

to SM

and with thanks to Buster & Polly

ISBN 0-936315-44-X

STARHAVEN, 42 Frognal, London NW3 6AG
books@starhaven.org.uk
www.starhaven.org.uk

Typeset in Dante by John Mallinson
Printed by CPI, 38 Ballard's Lane, London N3 2BJ

Contents

JOSEPINA

I

Grandma wanted Buddy dead. She took the framed photo off the wall and carried it to the little table by the window. Strips of plastic on the air conditioner slapped and clapped as the machine shuddered its cool breath through the apartment. The sun was just coming up on Flatbush.

Grandma took a pair of nail scissors and drew around the back of the frame so that she could remove the photograph. The picture showed her family, dressed formally, at the confirmation of her grandson. Once it was out of the frame, she opened the scissors as wide as she could and pressed one sharp point into Buddy's eye. With little snips, she edged around the image of his head, missing her daughter, her grandson and the priest.

She knew this would work. She knew she could bring about somebody's death. She'd done it with her own husband. Sal had been a lazy, violent idiot and she'd wished him dead for such a long time. Eventually she'd made it happen. One night, she had regained consciousness on the kitchen floor with her arm twisted uncomfortably beneath her and she'd made a decision. She'd pulled herself up and her eyes rested on a photo-booth image of Sal stuck to the refrigerator door. She lit the stove and, holding the photo by its corner, placed it over the flame, speaking in a whisper.

After that, it was only a matter of days before Sal was dead. Killed in an accident at the dockyard. He didn't have a job, so there was no good reason why he was hanging around that place that night. Two weeks later, some guy came to her home with an envelope of cash. He said that it was for her and she shouldn't go to the cops under any circumstances. She had no intention of talking to the police. She never had learned more than a few words of English and she hadn't yet met a policeman who spoke Sicilian. Besides, this was a blessing. She took the money and felt happier than she'd been for half a lifetime.

Grandma swept the pieces of Buddy's photo into her hand and walked into the kitchen. Cupping the fragments of the man she hated, her daughter's husband, she turned the knob on the stove and pressed the ignition. Each piece of paper disappeared into ash before it hit the flame. Noises from the street had started. Little brats going to school, cars honking. She'd better get ready. Maureen would be here soon, and she had to pretend to be asleep.

She mistrusted Maureen. She'd mistrusted all the carers her daughter had arranged for her, and Maureen was no different. Maybe even worse. She was cheerful and pushy. Trying to get Grandma to leave the apartment, clean out the back closet, engage in conversation. Sometimes Maureen even sang as she pushed the mop across the kitchen floor. Grandma found that if she slumped in the chair and pretended to sleep, Maureen was more likely to leave her alone. Grandma worried about stealing. Everyone steals from little old ladies. But she'd taken precautions. All the money she had she'd rolled into cigarette-sized tubes and sewn into the hems of skirts and jackets. And the jewellery she owned was stored at the bottom of a jar of flour on the kitchen shelf.

Later that morning the phone rang and Maureen brought it over to Grandma where she sat in the big chair. It was her daughter, Angela. Buddy was missing.

'Summa bitch, fucking sheet.' Grandma liked to say her curses in Italian but to swear in English.

'No, Ma,' said Angela. 'It's not a woman this time. He left his car keys and his wallet and everything. Just wasn't here when I woke up. He's disappeared.'

Grandma listened to her daughter's distress until the

conversation ebbed into silence.

'I don't know what to do, Ma,' said Angela. 'What shall I tell the kid?'

When Grandma hung up, she smiled. Then in huge vomiting gasps she started laughing. Laughing like she hadn't done in years. Maureen stuck her head in from the kitchen.

'Well, praise the sweet Lord, Josepina, it's great to see you laughin'. Thank you, God, for bringing joy into this house.'

A week later, with Buddy still gone, the cops had been called. They'd gone to Angela's house, searched through Buddy's stuff and started asking questions. Despite Grandma's relief that the bastard was out of the picture she was concerned that, in some way, this could lead back to her. She wanted to remove any trace of Buddy from her apartment. With Maureen's help, she moved the boxes from the overstuffed closet in the bathroom – all the things her children and grandchildren had asked her to mind over the years. Skateboards. Boxes of papers. A child's winter coat. She found a large envelope that Buddy had given her a few weeks before he disappeared. She'd objected at the time because the closet was stuffed and she was finding it difficult to close the latch on the door.

'Shut up, Ma,' he'd said. 'I pay for this apartment. If you don't like it, you can live on the street with the other old crazies.'

'Summa bitch' she'd muttered. He didn't pay for the apartment, Angela did.

As Maureen carried the boxes through to the living room, Grandma stayed in the bathroom with the envelope. She closed the door and sat down carefully on the toilet. Quietly and as gently as her old hands would allow, Grandma peeled the tape from the back of the package and looked inside. Some rolled up cash in an elastic band, a few slips of paper and about ten small bags of powder.

There was a commotion. She could hear Maureen yelling and some banging and smashing. With the bathroom door still shut, Grandma stood carefully and shuffled into the open, now almost empty, closet. She made herself small and pulled a few of the remaining clothes and towels over her before tugging the door shut.

She was there for an hour – maybe an hour and a half. When she was sure it was quiet, she pushed the door with her foot and crawled out. Her body was stiff. It took her a while to stand and she steadied herself by holding onto the sink 'til she was no longer dizzy.

The apartment was a mess. The table had been turned over, the drawers were hanging open, the chair cushions slashed. Maureen was lying on the kitchen floor.

Still holding the envelope, Grandma stepped cautiously towards the door, leaving sticky footprints from the kitchen to the coat-rack. She put on her coat and, for the first time in many years, left the apartment. She waited for the elevator thinking about what to do. She'd go and see Joe Longabardo. He was the guy. He had helped Sal before. He'd helped her own father, Frank. He owned a bar not too far away. He'd know what to do.

The street had changed. Brooklyn was noisy and busy – it always had been. But now she recognised few of the shops on her road and none of the people. It took her a long time to stumble down two blocks. People ignored her. She clutched the envelope inside her coat, which she held closed as if against a brutal wind.

When she got to the place where Joe Longabardo's bar was meant to be, she stopped. It was not the same. The shop was a café of some kind, selling pastries and coffee. There was a line outside and young people were talking to each other as they waited to be served.

Grandma crossed the road to the ballpark and sat herself down on a bench, facing the shop. She'd wait there for a while. Think what to do. Think how she might get a message to Joe Longabardo – or Sal perhaps. Sal. Even that bastard summa bitch was good for one thing, he always knew how to get out of trouble.

II

She was running as fast as she could, stumbling over rough ground, gasping for breath, all the time counting in her head – thirty-five, thirty-six, thirty-seven. She smiled wide as she leapt over a rotting tree stump, raising her arms like a dancer. She was going to beat her record of making it to Joe's Bar in less than a minute.

The moment her mother had asked her to fetch her father, Josepina had started running – and counting. She'd been sitting by that hot oven all day, taking care of the loaves and pizza dough that neighbours brought in to be baked. Her mother's words had freed her from the sweltering boredom and, without stopping for a second or giving her mother the chance to change her mind, she'd jumped up and ran.

Josepina's apron stuck to her bare legs, her skirt scrunched up her thighs and her hair was loose. She turned the corner and saw the men sitting in the shade outside the shack. Forty-eight, forty-nine. Her throat hurt, and tears were streaming sideways. She arrived and bent double, her hands pressing on her knees, panting. Fifty-two seconds. A new record.

'Where's the fire, Josie?' said Joe Longabardo. He was the only man standing in the group, moving around slowly to fill up their short glasses with liquid from an unlabelled brown bottle.

'Mama needs Father,' Josepina panted. 'I'm here to get him.'

The men laughed and Josepina's father tutted. He didn't like being the centre of attention or the butt of their jokes.

'You just sit there for a minute, girl,' said Joe. 'Your Papa will be along soon enough.'

Josepina flopped on the gravel-crunchy grass, face down, arms splayed. She tried to calm her breathing, so she could hear what the men were saying. They seemed to forget her immediately and went back to their conversation.

'The papers last for six months, no more than that. Then you have to start all over again,' said one man. Josepina didn't see who was talking. She kept her head down as she always did when grownups were discussing something important. You got to hear more if they didn't know you were listening.

'But once I get over there, I can send for the family. Mothers, fathers, in-laws, whoever. They have to consider every application. They have to. As long as we have the birth certificates, marriage certificates, all that stuff, they have to consider every application. You get to the front of the line.'

'How soon could you travel?' asked Joe.

The unidentified man was speaking quite urgently now, imploring the others. 'Let's say the marriage is next week, or this week even, we'd get to Palermo, do the paperwork – how long does that take? Maybe a week? We get the first boat we can. It goes from Palermo straight to New York America. Once we get there, we get the papers for the family to travel.'

Josepina heard a chair scraping gravel and looked up to see her father standing. Joe Longabardo put his arm around her father's shoulder.

'When he lays it all out like that, right? See what I mean, Frank?' Joe said.

Her father held his head down as he walked her back home, as if he was worried he'd trip or the ground would open up under his feet. He only said one thing to her before he went inside. 'You're getting married.'

Five days later, Josepina wore her mother's good dress to church. It was too big for her, but her mother had pinched in the back with pins. Even so, the thin fabric frequently slipped off her shoulders revealing her bony frame and causing her mother to wrench at the fabric – each time a little harder, as if it was Josepina's fault that it didn't fit. The dress, the trouble they'd gone to on her behalf, the grief she'd given them, causing them to beat her each day until she went along with the plan… It was all Josepina's fault.

She had officially met Biagio at her home a couple of days before. He'd not spoken to her once although he'd been friendly with her mother and father, even pinching her younger sister's cheek before he left. But she hadn't caught him looking at her at all, let alone saying a word. She'd decided she was going to hate him forever. Hate him even more than she hated her mother.

The church was fuller than it ever was on a Sunday. Biagio seemed to have many friends there and his brothers were crowded into the front row. The women sat at the back and all were happy and enjoying the celebration. Joe Longabardo had been passing around one of his brown bottles right there in the church. Everyone made a big show of giving Josepina coins to put in the little purse that her mother had sewn for her from a piece of cloth.

'A long and happy life to you both,' said one of her neighbours. Then, leaning down to whisper in Josepina's ear, 'keep hold of that purse. Anyone could pick up that purse, so don't take your eyes off it.'

Two days later, Josepina was in Palermo and it was not what she had expected at all. She'd spoken to her friends about it but, as none of them had ever been there, they'd filled her head with stupid stories of motor-cars, fancy restaurants and businessmen. It looked to her just like a bigger, dirtier version of Siracusa. Josepina cried for her sister and missed her father and would even have been happy to be back sitting beside the hot oven with her silent mother instead of with these strangers, who spoke loudly about things she didn't understand and whose every heavy footstep made her uneasy.

They were staying with Biagio's brother, Calogero, until the paperwork arrived. It was a small apartment with one bedroom where Calogero, Biagio and Josepina were sleeping, a kitchen where Biagio's other brother Sam slept and a bathroom that they shared with other families who lived on the same floor. Josepina kept herself busy, cooking and cleaning, trying to stay awake and occupied as long as she could so that she didn't have to go to bed before Biagio was asleep. Her mother had demonstrated the husband-and-wife nighttime activity in advance, going through the actions with Biagio for Josepina's instruction. But it was worse than what she'd witnessed when she had to be the one squashed flat on her back, in pain, barely able to breathe, for no good reason. And having Calogero watching from his bed on the floor beside them and grasping at himself as he did, made her sick.

Josepina didn't receive any messages from her family. When she urged Biagio to get word to them that she was OK, he didn't see the point. They had washed their hands of her, he said. She was his family now and it was better to think about the future, to make plans for America and forget about Siracusa. She was no longer a baby. She was going to be happy, he said, although she didn't know how he could have come to that conclusion.

They had been living in Palermo about a month when everything changed. Josepina was in her neighbour's apartment drinking cordial and using the big sink to wash clothes. She liked Maria, her neighbour, who was quite a few years older than Josepina but treated her like an adult, not like a stupid girl. Maria let Josepina accompany her to the market; they often cooked together and, when the jobs were done, Josepina would sit in Maria's apartment, listening open-mouthed to her stories which were full of gossip, insults and revenge. Maria even let her stay the night in her bed on the occasions when the men were drunk and fighting with each other.

Maria was sitting by the window, fanning herself with a paper plate and ranting on.

'I told her if I ever saw her again, I'd put a curse on her so that her tongue would cleave in two and everyone would see her for the snake that she is.'

Josepina sniggered. 'You wouldn't really?'

'I've done worse.'

There was a pounding on the door and Josepina jumped. Maria stood slowly, unalarmed, and went to open the door. It was Calogero. He rushed up to Josepina and grabbed her arm.

'You've got to come with me now,' he said, dragging her towards the door.

'Take your hands off the girl,' said Maria. 'This is my house.'

'Fucking shut it, Maria,' said Calogero. 'This ain't nothing to do with you.'

'Don't,' cried Josepina, but she was already in the hallway being half-dragged, half-carried back to their rooms.

'They got him,' said Calogero, slumping down into a chair and wiping tears from his eyes. 'Biagio's been arrested. This whole thing has been for nothing. He's in jail. And God knows when he'll ever get out.'

Josepina stood with her back against the wall and was silent. She was fuming. She didn't know what was going on, but she knew that her mother would blame her, her father would be angry and maybe now she was expected to have Calogero in bed with her. She hated them all so much that the rage tightened around her throat like a rope and she wondered if she'd ever breathe right again.

'The papers arrived for you and Biagio,' Calogero was raging. 'They're right in the drawer there with the tickets for the boat. And now he's locked up. What am I going to tell everyone? Your father has spent the money we gave him, I'm sure of it, so I can't even get that back. We just needed to get Biagio on the boat and he missed it – we only needed a few days. A few days. The fucking police got him.'

'I don't care what you tell Papa or Biagio or any of your stinking family,' said Josepina. Then all at once she was smiling, she stumbled on her words as if she was about the laugh. 'I'll go on my own.' She was free from her family, free from her husband and with paperwork to travel to America. 'I'm going to pack up my stuff from this shit hole and I'm going to stay with Maria until the boat leaves.'

'You can't leave without Biagio. He won't allow it. I won't allow it.'

'Fuck you,' said Josepina. 'You try one thing to stop me and I'll put a curse on you.' She loved how the swear words sounded, how her lips screwed up as she spat them out. It was the first time she'd said such things and would never have dared before

9

now. She felt strong.

'Fuck everyone and fuck you. I'm going to fucking New York America.'

III

The air had grown warmer over the hour they'd been sitting outside, the baby kicking her legs joyfully and wriggling on the blanket, and Josepina chuckling as she watched. Like a curtain going up to reveal something beautiful, the sun finally reached high enough in the sky that it was free of the surrounding buildings and, in one moment, the little backyard was flooded with American sunlight.

Josepina had spent much of her childhood outdoors and she felt it was right and healthy for her own daughter to enjoy the air as often she could. It was one of the things that had surprised her about living in New York – how much time people spent indoors. They talked about the weather and used it as an excuse to stay locked in, under cover and alone. She suffered the indignity of many young mothers – with every busybody neighbour offering advice and imagining they knew best for her child and for her. 'Let her cry.' 'Keep her covered up, she'll catch her death.' 'She needs to get used to other people, she's too clingy.' Josepina just looked down at her child and was able to ignore the unwelcome interference. Her daughter was perfect, and she knew what she was doing was right. The little girl, named Maria, slept on Josepina's chest throughout the night and, for Josepina, the human-hot weight of her child lying on her, as her own rib cage rose and fell in the gentlest of rocking motions, made her calm and happy.

Josepina had arrived in New York sick. She'd put her illness down to the long journey, sea sickness, homesickness. The family she was living with, Filippo and Connie Macca from the old country, had eventually forced her to acknowledge that she was having a baby. She'd tried not to think about it. It was unimaginable. She didn't look at herself as she washed and didn't spend any time considering what was ahead of her. When the pain started, and the baby came, she'd refused help from the doctor, only coming out of the bathroom when the baby was born, the placenta wrapped in paper, the umbilical cord cut with scissors and its little wound tied with thread. She'd wrapped the baby in a shawl and presented her to everyone who had been waiting anxiously in the next room.

'I need to write to Biagio and Papa,' she'd said as they cooed and marvelled over the pretty child and the suddenly confident mother. Josepina's reading and writing skills were not good and she asked one of the children of the household to write a letter for her. She had decided to call the baby Maria after her Palermo neighbour – it never crossed her mind to ask anyone's opinion or gather suggestions. When the nine-year-old son of Filippo and Connie Macca drafted up her words, he spelled the child's name Marie. It would be years before Biagio knew his first child's real name.

Little Maria was looking over to her mother. Josepina stooped to pick her up and swung her around to her breast. The baby fed well, snuffling like a little piglet, with one small pale hand holding the breast steady and the other clenching into a fist as she closed her eyes and drank, frowning slightly as she focussed on feeding. Josepina could feel the milk draining through her and sat back to enjoy the tickly relief. She closed her eyes too and let the sun wash her face.

She heard the screen door creak open behind her.

'Josie?' said Connie Macca. 'You want coffee or a water?'

'I'm fine.'

'Well, I'm going to bring mine out to you then.'

Connie was a round, warm-hearted woman and Josepina thanked God that it was this home that she had been sent to. They were friends of her husband's family, although they never mentioned how they knew him. Arrangements had been made for Josepina to stay with them and help Connie with her work while Biagio found a job. And, although Biagio never made it, Josepina had followed the plan and helped Connie sewing, cooking breakfast and doing the laundry each day.

'The baby's feeding very well,' said Connie. 'You can try her on some rice soon.'

'Perhaps,' said Josepina, her eyes still closed.

'Once she eats, it'll be easier for you to leave her when you have to. We can all help with her.'

'I'm fine.'

'But you'll need to have time away from each other,' said Connie and, finally Josepina opened her eyes and looked over.

'Why?'

Connie sighed a little – perhaps revealing her frustration or maybe bracing herself to deliver the bad news.

'Do you remember I spoke to you about the rich woman in Massachusetts? She's having her baby very soon and there's a job for you there. She needs you while your milk is good.'

Josepina was silent and trying to keep calm. She felt her eyes water and she closed them again to block out the information she knew was coming.

'You send the money to me for Maria and I'll be able to save some too for when you get back. Think of all the things Maria is going to need – clothes, furniture, medicine. You'll make money for that in Massachusetts and then be back to start your life with your daughter. Biagio might even be over here by then.'

'I don't care about Biagio,' said Josepina.

'I know it's hard,' Connie went on, 'but it isn't for forever. I did it when Benny was a baby. And look, we're all fine now. It's just a few months away.'

On the day she left, Josepina dressed Maria in a sweet little outfit and brushed her thin baby hair tenderly. The little girl was in good spirits and Josepina watched her bouncing back and forth in Connie's arms, hanging from one side to the other and smiling, boisterous and playful, as Connie carried her into the house.

Connie had made the arrangements for Josepina and given her advice about the job. 'If you're drying up, get a little puppy from the farm and let it lick you. It'll help bring the milk through.'

Josepina didn't cry openly on the train. She'd been through worse. And what good would tears do? This adventure made her feel like she was a proper adult at last, taking care of her responsibilities and getting the money she needed for her daughter. She spent her journey staring out of the window, daydreaming about what she'd buy for Maria and for herself once she'd saved up enough to come home.

The family in Massachusetts treated her well. She slept on a low cot in the new-born's room, had meals with the other servants and was even given clothes to wear. The baby was good. A sweet little boy who took to feeding with ease, slept well and caused Josepina no trouble. She played with him and cuddled him every day, speaking to him in her own dialect and singing songs from the old country as his eyes grew heavy after each feed.

Time passed easily and Josepina put on weight as she indulged in the rich food that the cook made for the family and they insisted on her eating to keep her strength up and her milk nutritious. She received letters from Connie Macca every now and again telling her that Maria was happy and doing fine. Josepina felt sure that she'd done the right thing. She cared for the little boy, pouring her love for her daughter into this substitute and watching him get stronger each day.

She was totally unprepared for Connie Macca's visit. One of the servants came into the nursery and told Josepina that she had a visitor and, at first, she thought there must have been some mistake.

'It's a Mrs Macca. She wants to see you.'

Josepina's heart started pounding. She laid her charge down in his cot and rushed out of the room and down the stairs. Connie was in the hallway, still wearing her coat and hat and clutching her pocketbook to her chest. The two women caught each other's eye as Josepina moved down the staircase and the look her friend gave her stopped Josepina in her tracks. She stayed on the steps, rigid.

'I'm so sorry,' said Connie, moving towards her. 'It's Maria.' Josepina's breathing turned to gasps, she slumped down and leant against the banister.

Connie was speaking softly. 'She became ill, she was such a weak little thing. She had diarrhoea and then just stopped eating. We got the doctor in. We didn't spare the expense, I promise you that.'

'When did this happen?'

'Three weeks ago,' said Connie. 'I wanted to tell you myself and it's taken me a while to make arrangements to get here.'

'Where is she?'

'We had a funeral. It was very beautiful, I promise. She was wearing the little white dress that Benny had for his christening. It's all done.'

Josepina's eyes went blank. She stayed where she was, refusing to respond to Connie's urging or the servant's attempts to cajole her. It took an hour of pleading before Connie gave up and was led to the front door by the servant.

'I can't see how she can blame me,' Connie was saying. 'I loved that girl like my own.'

The family was sympathetic but there was work to be done and eventually they asked for her to be taken back upstairs for the baby's afternoon feed.

Josepina took her place in the chair beside the window. As she was shaking and silent, another servant had been assigned to watch over her and she handed the baby to Josepina and positioned his lips on her breast. But the milk was gone. The baby tugged at her breast, became fractious and eventually was taken away.

They tried for two days to help Josepina feed the baby, bringing him to her every few hours and coaxing her to do her best to get the milk flowing. The baby was hungry, fed only on watered down cow's milk and was unable to latch on to the cracked nipples that no longer supplied any sustenance.

On the third day, Josepina was informed that she was no longer needed, another nurse had been employed. They'd give her money for a ticket home and would like it if she could be out of the house that evening.

In a daze, she took the train back to Brooklyn. She knew she couldn't stay with the Maccas now. Not after what they'd done. She wanted to go home. Her real home in Sicily. But before she did, she wanted to make Connie suffer. She wanted her to pay a price. She would have taken a knife to her throat, but she couldn't get away with that. She'd take some of Connie's hair and burn it, like her Palermo neighbour had taught her. Connie's stomach would fall out of her and all her shit and piss would cover the floor of that hateful house. Josepina's lips twitched as she imagined Connie's expression. She wouldn't know what was happening but Josepina would. She'd give Connie what she deserved and step right over her dying body, then get away and never return to this god-forsaken country again.

IV

Her favourite time of day was just before they opened. When Joe's Bar was empty but ready. Josepina and her sister cleaned down the tables, dragged in the bottle crates from the storeroom and wiped out the glasses. They were efficient. They made the place run like clockwork and, according to Joe Longabardo, who came in everyday to sit in his corner seat, the bar could rival any in Siracusa. Joe liked to wallow in the success of the place, which still had his name painted on a wooden sign above the door, although it was Josepina and Emmanuela who were in charge. Their father had bought the bar and the two rooms behind it that became their home, but not much had changed until Josepina had returned from New York.

Mysterious now to the neighbours who used to know her so well, Josepina had taken up the management of the bar within a month of returning. She oversaw the repairs, many of which she did herself, and roped her younger sister into helping serve the customers. She never answered questions about her time in America, so rumours formed. She had been thrown out for doing something unspeakable. She had been robbed and frightened out of her wits by some Chinese men. She had fallen in love with a villain whose father had threatened to have her killed. She had been bewitched and had fled back to the old country to undo a spell and escape a terrible destiny. Josepina was more confident now and few people had the guts to verify these tales with her.

'She'll skin you alive if you ask her,' they'd say. 'Just like she did that Chinaman.'

Josepina stood behind the bar and tied her apron tightly around her waist. Emmanuela knew the signal and went to unlock the door. There were already three men outside waiting for a drink. Direct from the fields, they took up their regular seats and were each given a short glass of wine. After a few sips, they relaxed, taking off the sweaty rags around their necks, unbuttoning their shirts and sinking into their chairs.

Josepina's mother made bread each day, returning to the old oven that used to be theirs morning and afternoon. She was known for her focaccia which was as soft as she was brittle. The sight of her balancing loaves on a wide plank of wood on her head as she hurried towards the bar drew people with her like they were hypnotised.

'Just in time,' said Joe Longabardo, following the woman in and helping her set the plank on the bar. 'I'm aching for food. Look at me,' he grabbed his belly with both hands. 'There's nothing left of me – a few hours more and I'll be a skelington.'

The men laughed and called out insults. Her job done, Josepina's mother retreated to the back rooms, muttering insults of her own about the jeering customers.

'It's coming,' said Josepina, ripping the bread and stuffing pieces into baskets.

'So is Saint Joseph's day,' said Joe, 'and by then I could be dead.'

Josepina laughed as she put a basket on each t[...]
Joe until last so that he continued wailing up until
she pushed a piece of bread into his face.

'Look at that,' Joe said to his audience, spluttering crumbs,
'she treats me like an old dog.'

'If you were an old dog you'd be tied up outside,' said
Josepina.

The bar was busy that evening. Someone was celebrating the
confirmation of their youngest daughter and wine flowed.
There were a few new faces and many regulars. Josepina shared
olives and bread and kept refilling the glasses, all the time
keeping track in her head of how much everyone had taken and
how much each of them owed her.

As the sun went down, Emmanuela lit candles. One of the
ways that Josepina had made things better was by extending the
hours the bar stayed open. In the past, the padlock was put on
the door when Joe Longabardo had drunk so much of his own
wine that he could no longer serve anyone else – that was often
before sundown. Now they could keep serving, keep everyone
drinking and keep taking their money.

Some men were getting rowdy at one end of the room, and
she saw her sister looking flustered as she tried to calm them. A
man pushed her out of the way and reached down to lean close
to another young guy yelling insults, spit flying from his lips.

Then, at the door, were two policemen. Everyone became
quiet, looking into their own drinks.

'What do you want?' said Josepina. 'Can I help you?'

The first policeman stepped past her and walked up to the
rowdy table. The man who had been so loud before was silent
now and stepped aside, hands behind his back like he was lining
up at church. The policeman ignored him, instead reaching over
to young guy, clasping one hand around his shoulder and pulling
him up.

'You're coming with me.'

There was no struggle. The young man was led out and the policemen took him away. His angry acquaintance watched them go, then darted out and down the road in the other direction.

After a moment's silence, Joe Longabardo, who had seemed to be dozing in his chair, piped up, 'if he's not going to drink his wine, it'd be a crime to let it go to waste.'

The men laughed and Josepina took the glass over to Joe, swaying it in front of him and forcing him to reach out to get it.

'You'd take the last sip from a dying man, you would.'

Emmanuela called Josepina over to the table that had just been emptied by the police. She pointed down. There was a parcel under the seat. A square of cloth tied with thin rope.

'That young one left this,' she said in her sister's ear.

Josepina bent down and inspected the package with her back to the room, peaking between the folds of the fabric. She saw the black muzzle of a gun and a grey shirt scrunched into a ball.

'Take this to the storeroom and hide it,' she whispered to her sister. 'Don't tell Mama.'

Once the candles burnt out and everyone had left, Emmanuela and Josepina swept the rubbish out onto the street and stacked the glasses into a wooden bucket for washing the following day. Emmanuela was tired and groaned 'good night' as she staggered off to the back of the building, letting her apron fall on the floor.

Josepina was still awake and alert. She knew the angry guy would be back.

She found another candle, lit it and stuck it in the still warm mound of wax on the table by the door. She pulled up a chair and reached into the pocket of her apron for her pouch of tobacco. She pinched at the tobacco, breaking it into small pieces before tucking it into her little pipe. She held the small corno pendant that hung around her neck and rubbed it between finger and thumb. Her eyes narrowed, and a smile crept onto her lips.

The door was still open, but it was so dark outside that Josepina didn't see the man until he was right in the doorway.

'We're closed,' she said without standing.

'I know,' he said, 'I left something here.'

Josepina twisted her head towards the candle to ignite the pipe. She was trembling slightly, and it took her longer than she would have liked. Leaning back in her chair, she stared at the man and puffed little balls of smoke up to the ceiling.

The man was hunting around the tables for his parcel.

'You won't find it,' Josepina said eventually.

'Do the police, have it?'

'Not yet they don't.'

At that, the man smiled. He walked over to Josepina and pulled up a chair, tucking himself close in to the table and leaning forward towards her.

'Let's have it then.'

Josepina moved slowly, lifting herself out of the chair, crossing the room and stepping behind the bar, her pipe balanced in her lips, bobbing slightly. She had her back to the man. She wanted to drag this out, show that she wasn't intimidated. She picked up two short glasses and tucked a bottle under her arm before returning to the table.

'I'm here for my stuff,' the man said, smirking.

'Yes, I want to talk to you about that,' she said. She poured wine into both glasses and shunted one towards him. 'You got a problem. I seen your guy being taken away. So, it seems to me that you need a new way to get your stuff looked after.'

'It seems to you?' the guy was amused. He picked up the glass, sniffed its contents and then with the other hand did a circling motion to hurry her along.

'I'm here all the time, every day, and I could look after things as they come and go.'

He was silent for a while. He looked around. He swigged at his drink. She refilled his glass and waited.

'First, I'm going to explain how this is going to work...' he said.

'No,' she sounded louder than she meant to. 'I have the stuff. I am the one explaining.'

V

Biagio's return to Siracusa was treated like the homecoming of a war hero. The bar was decorated with paper streamers, a big meal was prepared with cakes, cheeses, breads and pastries packed tight into baskets and struggling for space with the bottles lined up along the bar. Josepina's parents were excited, inviting everyone over and dressing up for the occasion. Josepina herself was quiet. She carried on with her work and left her mother to make the arrangements. Her Mama seemed to have the enthusiasm for it. Besides, Josepina was suspicious about how the arrival of her husband was going to impact her life at the bar, her side-line business and what she'd soon be facing after dark in the marital bed.

Biagio was happy to be home, he said, but he seemed shy about the fuss and, once the initial cheering, tears and hilarity from his family and in-laws had died down, he was happier in a seat by the door, watching the party and cradling his hands around his glass of wine as if it was providing warmth.

He stayed seated until most of the guests had left and then called Josepina over.

'Where do we live now?' His voice was softer than she remembered, exhausted-sounding.

'We all live here,' she replied. 'Did Mama tell you? She's set up a bed for you in their room. I'm in the other room with my sister.'

Biagio nodded. She wiped down the table in front of him and for a moment felt some sympathy.

'We can all talk about it tomorrow,' she said.

But they didn't talk about it. The next day, Biagio visited one of his brothers and was working with him by the end of the week. A few days later, he moved with Josepina into a home of their own closer to Siracusa town. One bedroom, a living space with a kitchen and an area out back to plant herbs and vegetables and to get the sun.

Josepina's mother resisted at first but, with a promise that

Josepina would be at the bar every day as usual, it was agreed. Emmanuela wept as her sister packed up her few belongings.

'Don't be a baby,' Josepina pinched her young sister's cheeks and smiled into her wet eyes. 'I'll see you every day and you'll have so much more room in bed now.'

Their life settled into a routine. Even after the babies came, they stayed in that apartment. Josepina and Biagio both went to work each day, Josepina taking her daughters with her to the bar. The elder girl, Angela, would sit behind the bar and play; the other, Sadie, would be strapped to her hip, Josepina's apron stretching over her chubby legs, tucking her in close to free herself to pour wine, exchange money and wipe down tables.

Josepina had hoped that her mother would help take the girls now and again. But her mother showed little interest. She was distracted and, even at the christening which they held as a joint celebration when Sadie was six months old and Angela three, she left early without explanation. Emmanuela was different. She loved her nieces and was happy to play with them, cuddle them and feed them little bits of bread dipped in milk or oil, wiping their chubby chins afterwards with the corner of her sleeve. She kept Angela overnight sometimes in the bed that she had shared with her sister. And the little girl followed her around the bar, helping where she could by swatting at flies with a cloth and picking the wax off the tables, so serious in her efforts that Joe Longabardo would laugh and remark that Angela was the new boss now.

Emmanuela was disappointed when Angela was old enough to want to go and play on her own. The lively girl would run from the bar to where her father was working at a farm nearby, ducking under fences and avoiding the livestock to surprise her Papa amongst his friends and brothers. He always made a big fuss of her.

'She's here at last,' he'd say, gathering her up onto his shoulders, 'the heavy work can start now. Get Angela that hammer and she'll show you how to do it.'

Josepina enjoyed seeing her husband with their daughters. At night he insisted on having one or both on his knee as he ate his dinner.

'It's not teaching them right manners,' she scolded but she served them, nonetheless. The chair would creak as they clambered over him and it was only when it threatened to break that she insisted they all sit down properly before someone got hurt.

Time in bed alone with Biagio was better than it had been. She was more comfortable and although she still didn't enjoy the sweating and thrusting, she liked the conversations they'd have, just the two of them, after it was over. He'd tell her about his plans once the crops came in and how they should take the girls up to Palermo to meet his brother's growing family. He spoke of them all dressing up and riding the train like smart people.

'Nobody will say we're just country idiots,' he said.

She stitched two pretty dresses for the girls for the impending trip. They looked so beautiful that when Biagio first saw them together with their hair tied back, faces shining, holding out their skirts like little dolls, he got teary-eyed and declared that they should use the money he'd saved for a family photo portrait instead. They'd get to go to Palermo soon enough, but he never wanted to forget this moment.

The photography shop was hot and young Sadie had been crying right up until the moment the elderly photographer ushered them into the studio. A painted background of Mount Etna with a blue sky and unlikely bright green coastline caused the whole family to go silent. The resulting picture, which they bought two copies of – one for the family home and one for the bar – showed them all looking a little alarmed. Sadie had her eyes closed and her lips in a tight pout. Angela was looking up at her father intently. Josepina and Biagio stared forward blankly. They were thrilled with the result.

Emmanuela thought it was the best photograph she'd ever seen and made sure she spat on it a couple of times before it went up on the wall of the bar, so the devil didn't notice its striking beauty.

Just before her fifth birthday, Angela lost all interest in going to the bar, or visiting her father at work or running around the countryside. Many days, Josepina had to stay at home with her because the child was too ill to eat or get out of her bed. Her parents were worried and called in help from a neighbour. The old woman held her hand on the girl's head and remarked that she didn't seem hot. She looked into her eyes and throat but saw nothing to account for the change in her.

'Let her sleep,' she'd said. 'It'll be over soon.'

Nights were troublesome. Biagio and Josepina sat watching their daughter breathing lightly, her face pale, with grey shadows under her eyes. Her lips were wet and dark red, puckering with effort at every breath.

'We need a real doctor,' said Biagio. 'We need to find money for a real doctor.'

Josepina had a very bad feeling about what was going on.

One morning, when Biagio had left for work and Sadie was napping, she gathered a bowl of water and a jug of oil and took them into the bedroom. Angela was asleep on the double bed. She was sweaty and had kicked off the blanket that had been tucked in so carefully moments before.

Josepina placed the bowl on the floor and held the jug of oil high, tipping it slowly to let a small drop fall onto the waiting pool. The water shuddered, and the oil separated into droplets before coming together in a teardrop shape. Josepina watched closely to see if there would be any change. In time, she picked up the bowl and jug and returned them to the kitchen. She had all the information she needed.

She waited until she had fed Sadie that night and tried to get some nourishment into the still drowsy Angela, before taking Biagio outside to talk. It was a clear night and the outside garden seemed brighter than it had been indoors.

'Someone has put the malocchio on little Angela,' she

blurted out.

'Who would do that? Why would anyone do that?'

'Jealousy. Anger. Hate.' Josepina explained how she'd carried out the oil and water ritual and how the sign was clear. The girl was cursed.

Biagio cried out. He raged against everyone they knew. They'd already lost one baby in America and now a second was about to die. He kicked at the wall until the bricks started to crumble. He yelled and shook his fists. Josepina just watched. It was comforting to see someone expressing what she was feeling. The upstairs neighbours opened their window and peered out but closed it quickly once they caught his attention and he screamed up at them in his despair.

'This isn't going to happen. Not again,' he said. With purpose, Biagio walked into the bedroom and picked up the sleeping Sadie and handed her to Josepina.

'Take her.'

'What are you doing?' Josepina wrapped up the toddler in a blanket and sat with her as she watched Biagio, busying himself in the kitchen. He took the coins from his pocket and laid them on the counter. He washed his face in the sink. Finally, he came over to kiss his youngest daughter. After pressing his lips on her forehead, he took her hand and let her squat fingers grip his thumb.

'Pappi loves you, little one.'

In the same tender way, he kissed the top of Josepina's head.

'Everything's going to be fine,' he said. He went into the bedroom and closed the door.

Josepina sat for as long as she could, watching the door. There was no sound. Eventually, as the sun was coming up, she tucked Sadie onto the soft chair and stepped forward to open the door. What she saw didn't surprise her. It was what she understood from the moment she'd seen that oil form into the shape of an eye. She knew the family had been cursed and there was little she could do to stop the impending disaster.

Angela was sitting up. She was smiling.

'I'm hungry, Mama,' she said.

Beside her Biagio was still. Lying on his back, with his mouth open and his eyes staring at the ceiling. He looked the colour of cement. It was early and Josepina could hear the birds starting their morning conversations. She put her hand to Biagio's cheek and whispered, 'thank you'.

VI

It was 18 months after Biagio's death that Josepina met Sal. He'd come into Joe's Bar with a group of rowdy friends. He was on a visit home from America and his friends were keen to introduce him to Josepina, one of the few other people they knew who had ever left Sicily.

'She hated it,' one of them said.

'That's not true,' said Josepina, flustered under the hot focus of the stranger's smile.

'Maybe you just needed someone to show you around,' Sal said.

Sal was loud and charismatic. His friends made him the centre of attention and he filled the role effortlessly, telling stories, laughing and joking. He was playful and entertaining. It got late, and they bustled him out of the bar. Josepina walked to the door to lock up, watching the gang staggering down the street into the dark. Then Sal turned and, in a comedy stride like a street performer, with his friends yelling behind him, he paced his way back to Josepina and asked her to see him the next day.

'I'm working,' she said.

'Well, I'll see you here then.'

Sal got on with everyone. With her kids, with her sister and parents and especially with Josepina herself. When the time came for him to return to Brooklyn, she had already decided that if he asked her to join him she'd go.

He lived in a two-bedroom apartment in Flatbush, and the new family settled in well. Sal was a sociable guy, and there was barely a day that someone wasn't stopping by to visit or dragging him out with them to meet friends. The flat had a feeling of Joe's Bar at times and Josepina enjoyed keeping everyone fed and pouring drinks, always bustling people out as the sun rose, before she had to get the girls ready for school.

The change in Sal took place over such a long time that she could never pinpoint exactly when he had become a different man. The girls were teenagers and spending less time at home. The quietness in the flat was unnerving but it was the contrast in her once-playful husband that preyed on Josepina's mind. Sal rarely got up during the daylight hours any more; he'd lie on the couch in the living-room with the TV buzzing as she tiptoed around. People didn't come over like they used to, and she avoided inviting friends of her own. She was embarrassed of Sal, passed out and snoring, sweating onto the cushions, impossible to move.

Angela had started dating Sal's nephew, Buddy, and Sadie had taken a job on the weekends at Sal's sister's restaurant. Yes, Sal's family were kind to them, but they never wanted to know Josepina's concerns. They tutted at her when she gave excuses for Sal's absence at family gatherings or changed the subject when she hinted about his violent temper.

She sat watching Sal, tasting her disappointment turning into anger. He had so little interest in life, let alone in her. When they ever spoke, she was manic – trying to fit as much into the conversation as she could before he disappeared into his stupor. Her sister was coming to Brooklyn for a visit. She was travelling with Joe Longabardo who had finally secured a visa and a place to live with a cousin in Queens. Emmanuela was going to accompany the old man and take the opportunity to catch up with her sister and nieces. Josepina was excited to the point of tears. She wanted things to be perfect and she nagged and prodded Sal to get himself together.

'Can't you see I'm not well, woman?'

'You're never well anymore.'

'Can you imagine what it's like? To feel bad all the time and my own wife has no sympathy.'

Josepina decided to pick her sister and Joe up from the airport and help them on the bus out to Queens. It would give her a chance to see both of them without Sal and she could then pick her moment to invite her sister home. Maybe Sal would rally and put on an act for that at least. Josepina worked out the route from JFK to Flushing with her neighbour and even jotted down a few phrases in American in case she needed to ask for help.

She was at the airport so early and had watched so many people pop through the arrivals door that she was getting drowsy. When her sister finally appeared, she almost didn't recognise her. Emmanuela looked like an old woman as she struggled with luggage and led an even older Joe beside her. She and Josepina embraced and smiled at each other, but Emmanuela was quiet. Even once on the bus, with Joe Longabardo snoozing in the seat in front of them, the sisters were silent. Josepina imagined Emmanuela must be exhausted after such a long trip and the stress of being on an airplane for the first time.

The house in Flushing was in a row that all looked alike, the type of houses a child would draw. Two windows at the bottom, two at the top and a door right in the middle. It took the three of them a while to make it from the bus stop to 164th street and, by the time they got close, they could see Joe's cousin standing on the porch watching frantically.

They were welcomed with a feast. Food and wine and lots of hugging. Josepina tried to offer her help. 'We use paper plates' Joe's cousin said, 'so we never have to wash the dishes.'

'It's another world,' said Joe, impressed.

When Joe's cousin and his wife suggested that Josepina stay the night rather than trying to get back to Flatbush so late, she agreed. She'd slip in with Emmanuela like the old days.

But they didn't fall into easy conversation like they used to. Josepina pushed her sister for details of the family, the bar and the neighbours and friends.

'Nothing's changed,' said Emmanuela. 'If you miss everything so much why don't you visit?'

'Are you upset with me?'

'No. It's not you. It's just that it's so difficult now. Mama has become so much worse since Biagio died and you left.'

'I thought she wanted me to leave. She never said I should stay.'

'She hates everything. Hates everyone. Just spends all her time on her own. Doesn't even go to church anymore.'

'I could arrange to come for a visit with the kids.'

'No, don't,' said Emmanuela. 'I was just saying that because it was easier for me when you were there. Mama wouldn't welcome a visit.'

The women were silent.

'She's said some pretty terrible things about you,' said Emmanuela after a while. 'Made me start to think that she had something to do with the malocchio on Angela.'

'But why would she do that?'

'She's just so full of anger towards you.'

'What did I do?'

'I don't know, Josie. It doesn't make any sense.'

They went quiet again, and eventually Emmanuela fell asleep. Josepina lay awake thinking about how things had turned out. It didn't come as much of a surprise to her that her mother hated her. Maybe she always had. It wasn't nice to hear those words, but in a strange way it was a relief. Things did actually make more sense than Emmanuela knew.

Josepina didn't feel like sleeping or staying in this strange house any longer. She stepped out of bed carefully and tucked the blanket back around her sleeping sister. She got dressed, found her bag and coat on the rack in the hallway and let herself out.

The street was deserted. The streetlights were still glowing and yet she could tell that the sun was coming up and another day was beginning.

VII

One after the other, they were trying to pull the wool over her eyes. It had started with Buddy. After Sal's death, his nephew, now her daughter's husband, had assumed the role of head of the family. It wasn't long before he'd started taking liberties. He would come in to check on Josepina, he'd say, but she knew that he was poking around, seeing what was there of value, sizing up the place, which was bigger than the apartment he lived in with Angela. As if Josepina needed checking on. No man had ever done anything for her, never given her anything, even furniture.

Buddy had opened a joint bank account for Josepina, so he could keep her money 'safe and sound', jumping on a single incident where she'd forgotten to pay some bills to take control. 'Let him help, Ma,' Angela said. 'This has really got out of hand.'

Josepina didn't have a choice, but she wasn't happy about it. What did it matter if the electricity had been out for a couple of days? She'd lived for most of her childhood without electricity and hadn't come to any harm. And it was the summertime anyway when it happened. But she couldn't object. Angela was pregnant and had become more demanding, relating every issue back to whether it was stressing her out and her nerves could hurt the baby.

Josepina had tried to make things easier for Angela, always. She went to the store for her when she could, picking up things she knew were good for the baby growing inside her. Once Angela's belly started getting so round that she could only fasten one button on her coat, Josepina decided to take a few precautions. Even though her own mother had died a few years before, she knew that a curse could remain long after anyone responsible for it was in their grave. Josepina went into the haberdasheries on East 18th Street. She chose a small piece of red ribbon and frayed the end. She'd attach this to Angela's coat to give her the appearance of being scruffy, less than perfect and not something the devil should take an interest in.

It was as she was paying for the ribbon that she noticed Buddy, leaning over the counter opposite, engrossed in a conversation with a young woman. He had her hand in both of his and was pulling her towards him as she giggled and wrestled away.

'You can't resist me forever,' he said and then swung around to leave. He came face to face with Josepina.

'You?' he said, unfazed. 'We seeing you for dinner tonight?'

Josepina was silent. Buddy shrugged and walked towards the door to the street. Before he left, he yelled over to the girl who was still watching him.

'See you soon, beautiful.'

The baby shower was held at Josepina's home. Angela and Buddy didn't want to tempt fate or take any risks by arrogantly storing baby furniture or clothing at their apartment. Emmanuela and her daughters arrived first and helped push back the sofa and bring chairs in from the kitchen. It was nice to have them there. Josepina hadn't seen as much of her sister as she had hoped once she had come to live in the U.S., but it was a long journey from Brooklyn to New Jersey and, as neither of them had learned to drive, they had to rely on one of their children to take them. Sadie came in from Long Island and was already sulking. As everyone else moved furniture and peeled plastic off the plates of food, she sat flicking through a magazine she had brought with her.

Angela's friends arrived with food and gifts, and some of Josepina's neighbourhood friends came too. By three o'clock it was getting crowded and noisy. Josepina recognised one of the young women as the girl from the haberdashery and peered at her. The young girl seemed oblivious, didn't pick up that she wasn't welcome and even thanked Josepina and kissed Angela before she left, taking with her a piece of cake wrapped in kitchen paper.

A couple of days later, Buddy stopped by to look through the gifts. Josepina made him coffee and would have spat in it if Buddy hadn't been sitting right behind her in the kitchen as she poured it.

'It's the chance of a lifetime,' he was ranting, eyes darting around and fingers drumming the plastic tablecloth. 'There's an investment needed but we have that covered with the money in the bank account. I've put in the work for this and they've seen it at last. They're going to take a leap of faith and let me have my own territory.'

Josepina wasn't listening. She stared at Buddy and hoped he'd choke on the hot coffee.

'Who was that girl?' she said eventually.

'Oh please. Is that what you're worried about? I'm talking about how we're all going to get rich. I'm thinking about our future. Can't you focus for a moment? Have you heard a word I've said?'

'You've got a new job?'

'No, I'll be working for myself,' he was frustrated. 'That's what I'm saying. We'll be working for ourselves.'

'Piece of sheet,' Josie muttered as she turned to wipe the kitchen counter.

'Ma, we've got a chance here. Think about it. This apartment is the base; we can store some of the product here, but nobody but me will ever come to get things or drop things off. That I guarantee. So, you don't have to worry. I'll give you a cut of everything I make. You'll have more money than you know what to do with. I'm taking the risks on the street. You just find a good place to keep it all hidden when I need you to. I know you can do that. You're a great little squirrel, Ma.'

Buddy took her hand with both of his and held it up to his face as if he was nibbling at a nut.

'I just need you to be the little squirrel.'

Josepina snatched away her hand.

'The girl in the shop?'

Buddy laughed. 'Ok, ok. I won't see the girl. You drive a hard bargain, old woman. But you'll do it, right?'

Josepina didn't comment. But she refilled Buddy's cup of coffee and they both knew that meant she was coming around to the idea.

VIII

Grandma sat and waited. After a while, she forgot what she was waiting for, but she knew it was important and assumed that it would come back to her soon enough. The Brooklyn ball park was lively. The line of people in front of the coffee shop had all been served and now she could see the workers inside wiping down the counter and talking to each other.

She was fed up with everyone trying to get one better. She didn't trust that Maureen. Why couldn't she choose her own cleaner? She would put her foot down with Angela. That girl shouldn't forget who was in charge. Why, if she'd spoken to her own mother in that voice, she'd have received a slap around the head that would have made her ears ring.

A woman pushing a stroller moved towards Grandma, looking concerned. She bent down to talk to her and said something in a calm voice that Grandma didn't understand. Grandma smiled and stuck up her thumb. As if that was the answer she was looking for, the woman nodded and moved on. Busybody.

Was she waiting for someone? Grandma had the envelope and she put it on the bench beside her. No address. No stamp. She can't have been going to the post office.

There was a young couple on the bench at the other side of the park. They were affectionately staring at each other and kissing. Grandma wondered if she had ever been in love. Maybe with Biagio, but not at first. No, she'd hated him at first. But familiarity grew over time, or a relief when things had settled down and she got used to how life was going to be. It wasn't love. She had loved her babies, but love for a man? That was a rich woman's luxury.

She should probably go soon, she thought. 'I'm going to need to put on dinner, maybe make some focaccia for a change.' She sat thinking about the ingredients she had in the icebox and what she could turn it into to keep Biagio and the kids happy.

Then she saw Connie Macca. She was walking along pushing

a bicycle. For a moment, Grandma wanted to call out to her but, even though she had forgotten who she was meeting, she was sure it couldn't be Connie. She had hated her after she let little Maria die. Had wished her dead. And yet, here she was, pushing a bike and talking to herself, her big fat arse swishing to and fro as she went past.

It was a warm afternoon, yet Grandma tucked her coat around her as she sat there. She kicked at the pigeons that gathered at her feet. It wasn't so bad here. There was a lot to entertain her as she waited. There was a guy that looked like Sal in the coffee shop now, sitting at a bar against the window with a briefcase. Sal with a briefcase? Yeah, that was just like him, spending money on himself on things he didn't need. Never a care for the family. She put her hand up to her jaw automatically and gave it a rub. He always hit her on the left side. For a while she had tried to cover up bruises with makeup. But what was the point, really? You'd think nothing of seeing a friend with a black eye. Or the woman in the butcher's shop with a broken nose. Often, it's easier not to ask. Everyone knows, and the excuses are so unconvincing that it's better not to bring it up.

Two men walked by. Buddy and a friend, she thought. She stood up, but they ignored her. They were talking and laughing. Maybe it wasn't him. No, obviously it wasn't him. He should be home at this time, what with the baby coming and everything.

Grandma sat back down and let her eyelids sag. Had she ever felt so tired? Even working at Joe's Bar hadn't taken so much out of her. Those rowdy customers all demanding her attention and that fool Joe sitting in his chair adding to the chaos. 'Idiot,' she giggled under her breath. She should have a word with him about his tab. He couldn't go on expecting free drinks for life just because that shack had once belonged to him.

Perhaps she should leave soon. No one would blame her. She'd been here for hours and they obviously weren't coming. She opened her eyes and saw a policeman walking towards her with one of the guys from the café.

The cop stood over her and spoke. It startled Grandma and

she looked around for something she recognised, the person who was supposed to be here with her. She was in trouble. She knew that much. Her mother had probably sent the cop. No, that couldn't have happened. Her mother was dead. Thank God.

'Italiano?' the cop was saying as he helped her up and guided her down the street. Grandma looked behind her at the package on the bench. Did that matter? Should she go back and get it?

'Io parlo italiano,' the cop said. 'Come ti chiami?'

Grandma smiled. She'd go with him, but she wouldn't say a word. Not a word. She was like a rock. Always had been. If she was in trouble, she'd get out of it herself. She was unsure about what was going on, couldn't place where she was, but she was certain about that. She could look after herself.

VERONICA

I

Of course, London hadn't changed. It had only been two years. But the famous buildings and low-hung ceiling of sky made Veronica feel like she was on a film set. Everything looked smaller than she remembered, the colours muted, not quite real.

She pointed out Battersea Power Station to her kids as the train went by. 'It's like a kitchen table turned upside down, can you see?' The children had been bouncing around the carriage with excitement but were now transfixed, noses pressed against the window, sensing that after a six-week journey this was the moment of truth. 'We'll get a black cab from the station.'

'Can I sit on the pull-down seat?' said her eldest daughter, Natalie.

'You remember that, do you?'

'Of course.'

Natalie started getting her coat on and pulling down the other jackets for Alice and little Alexander. None of the coats was going to be warm enough for London; Alex's only came to his waist. That summer Britain had experienced a record-breaking heat wave, but Veronica's homecoming coincided with the return of October clouds and rain, and the kids had complained of being cold from the moment their ship had docked at Southampton. They'd have to go shopping tomorrow. Get into the flat, settle in, then make a proper plan. Veronica needed to get the kids into a school as soon as possible and reconnect with her agent. She needed work first and foremost and God knows who was casting. She was completely out of the loop. She hadn't given herself much time to make any career plans, she had just wanted to leave Australia, so she had. People assumed that she was heartbroken after her best friend Bobbi had drowned, and there was truth in that. But actors loved gossip and Veronica's decision to return to London with the kids but without her husband had given everyone in the company something to talk about.

They had a suitcase each – even five-year-old Alex carried a little one – and their jackets buttoned up tightly. When the taxi dropped them in front of the mansion block, she smiled at the tableaux they made, Veronica, Natalie, Alice and Alex, lined up in height order, looking up at the building expectantly, as if they were about to burst into a musical number.

'Hello home,' Veronica sang out. The block of flats was a bit run-down and the corridors inside as cold as the street. They took the lift to the third floor and tried their key in the lock. When it didn't work, Veronica rang the bell.

Mrs Terzi opened the door, a toddler on her hip. She didn't seem surprised to see Veronica. But she also didn't seem happy.

'Hello darling,' said Veronica, pushing forward. 'I wasn't expecting you but it's good to see you. What a journey. Seems the key doesn't work.'

The suitcases stayed in the entrance hall and the children stood beside them as Mrs Terzi explained to Veronica that yes, she had received news that they were returning from Australia but she had been paying the rent and the flat was hers now. Her husband would be home from work soon and he'd explain everything.

There was no time to fully take in the information before Veronica was screaming at Mrs Terzi. The children bawled as their mother yelled, but the young Turkish woman was unflustered. Veronica could feel her throat closing up as she moved from yelling to pleading. Veronica had left Mrs Terzi, her cleaning lady, in charge of the flat while they were away but they were back now, and it was time for her to hand it over.

'Where is your husband?' Mrs Terzi asked.

'What difference does that make? You shouldn't be here.

This is my home. What the fuck is going on? You can't do this.'

'You should call your husband.'

Veronica made a big show of taking her address book out of her handbag, struggling with the zip, locating the book and striding towards the phone on the table in the entrance hall. 'You will not get away with this.'

She sat and waited until Mrs Terzi had gone into the kitchen before picking up the receiver. The dial tone was loud now the room was silent. A solemn, unsympathetic buzz, not the pipping tone she had grown accustomed to. It reminded her she was back in England, and she felt like a stranger.

'Are you going to call Daddy?' Alice asked.

'Please sit and be quiet. I'm going to sort this out.' Veronica wasn't going to attempt to track down Alan in Adelaide. Whatever time it was over there, it was unlikely her husband would pick up the phone. What could he do anyway? She also knew there was a risk of his secretary answering and she wasn't sure how she was going to explain the situation. Hardly a triumphant welcome home. No, she'd think about that later. She dialled her friend, Bruce.

Bruce was kind but firm. He mentioned something about possession being nine-tenths of the law and now they were in the flat they had to stay. With the locks changed they might never get in again. The landlord probably wouldn't help because Veronica had been sub-letting which she knew was against the rules and it was Friday afternoon now anyway, so she'd not be able to talk to them until after the weekend. Bruce was coming around to the flat. They'd make a plan. As she listened to his instructions, Veronica cried softly, and Alex crawled into her lap to comfort her. After promising that she wouldn't leave the flat before Bruce arrived, Veronica put down the phone and sat stroking Alex's silky hair, watching his eyelids closing.

Then she flicked through her address book again, picked up the phone and dialled.

'Felix?' her voice was warm and friendly. 'It's Veronica Craig. I'm back. Oh yes, just arrived. Of course, I'm available – I'm in good voice, never been better – you know what I'd love just about now? I'd love a handful of gigs. Let me give you my new phone number. Throw something my way, dear heart, will you? Got to keep the wolf from the door.'

For the next three weeks, Veronica gathered advice from friends, kept vigil in the flat and argued with Mrs Terzi. She managed to get the kids into a nearby school even though it was mid-way through the term and she sent them off each day in their new school uniforms and unfamiliar text books. Natalie and Alice were uncomplaining; they were used to being the new girls and had lost count of how many schools they'd been to at that point. Alex cried for a week, but Natalie looked after him. Natalie had been very attached to her little brother even before the drowning accident. They'd had a crazy Australian nanny who had beaten the kids way beyond what they could have deserved, and Natalie had been the one who had shown Veronica the bruises up and down Alex's little legs and bottom. They fired the nanny and Natalie had taken over much of the baby-sitting since then. She was mature for a ten-year-old. The kids went off to school each day and at night, when Veronica was out singing, they played with Mrs Terzi's little boy, watching telly together when the cartoons came on.

Veronica made every effort to make Mrs Terzi uncomfortable. Although she was sleeping with her kids in one room, she spread their things out across the kitchen and hallway, so they couldn't be ignored. She kept the radio on loud, even when the baby was supposed to be napping. But most of all, she nagged Mrs Terzi and pleaded with her to leave. Sometimes the bickering turned into full scale rows.

One day, Mrs Terzi called the police. She was hysterical by the time the two uniformed cops arrived.

'She's hurting my baby, she wants to kill my baby,' she was crying.

The policemen barely registered what she was saying. They addressed their questions to Veronica.

'This is my flat and she's squatting.' Veronica played the role of the reasonable party with confidence. 'I've been advised to live here while my legal team sorts things out. It's unbearable.'

'You haven't hurt the baby then?' The cop appeared to be smirking and he hadn't written anything in his notebook.

'Of course not. This woman is a squatter in my house and I admit we've argued but can you imagine what I'm going through?'

The cops asked both women to calm down and said that they didn't want to be called again to this flat.

As Veronica showed them to the door, one of the cops leaned towards her. 'We see this all the time with the Turks,' he said. 'Illegal immigrants most of them.'

Veronica thanked them both as they went out.

Mrs Terzi hadn't stopped crying.

'My baby has bruises. I know you've been hitting my baby.' With that, she stood the little boy on the table and pulled down his trousers. The baby had a big nappy, but the black and blue marks were clear, all down both legs.

'I don't know what you're talking about,' said Veronica, flustered to see the little wounded legs. 'That's got nothing to do with me.'

She spent the rest of the night in the bedroom with her kids. 'I don't think you should play with the Terzi boy anymore,' she told them.

It was only a day or two later that Mr Terzi told Veronica they were leaving. They had a list of demands. Bruce was there with Veronica when Mr Terzi read out his conditions. They'd be allowed to keep one room padlocked for their stuff which they'd come and collect in a month or two. They would be given money back for the rent they'd paid for that month – for all the time that Veronica and the kids had been there. Nobody shook hands, but the agreement was made. By the next evening the padlocked room was filled, and the Terzis left.

Veronica and the children danced around the flat. She

squeezed each of the kids and told them how brave they'd been. Everything was going to be better now. They looked in the other empty bedrooms and chatted excitedly about what they were going to do and who was going to sleep where. Then Veronica sent Natalie off to bring back fish and chips to celebrate. Alice and Alex wanted to go with her and Veronica could hear the three of them chattering and laughing as they raced down the stairs.

With the flat quiet and empty at last, she sat on the floor in the kitchen with her back against the wall. She looked around. There was a lot to do before their belongings arrived from Australia the following week. The place was dirty. Unrecognisable from the happy home they'd lived in before they'd moved. But it was theirs again. She stroked the floor with both her hands, moving them back and forwards, caressing the boards.

'Hello home,' she sang softly.

II

'If you don't care what you look like, then who else will?' Judith was balancing on the dressing table with her legs stretched out to a little black chair. She wore fishnet tights that, if anyone chose to inspect closely, had been repaired once or twice. She had a pair of nail scissors in one hand and was poking a hole in a satin bra.

'He likes to see my nipples through my blouse and I'm happy to oblige.'

Carefully, so as to avoid the ribbon that was threaded through the material to create a heart and arrow motif, she snipped a circle that she felt would be just big enough.

'It seems a bit pervy to me,' said Florentina. 'And a waste of good lingerie.'

'You, my dear… ' but Judith didn't finish her statement. She was working on the other bra cup and concentrating to ensure they were symmetrical. Showing off nipples was only effective if they stood up perfectly, like girls in a chorus line.

As the youngest in the Sheffield theatre company, at the start of her career, Veronica was squashed into a space at the end of the mirror. One arm touched a rack of costumes and the other was held uncomfortably to avoid bumping Florentina, who was drawing her face on.

The tannoy attached to the wall kept the three of them up to speed on the show. The stage manager's announcements interjected periodically in a thick Yorkshire accent didn't cause any reaction from the three actresses. They had time.

There was a swift knock on the door and the Company Manager, Mary, stuck her head in. 'All cast on stage after the curtain,' she said.

'I've got a date,' said Judith. 'Is it absolutely necessary?'

'Sorry to bugger up you getting laid, Jude,' said Mary. 'Alan Tomlinson is in. He wants to meet everyone.'

Veronica held down her smile. She'd met Alan before. She had an inkling that he'd recommended her for this job. The call had come out of the blue and, as she hadn't even got an agent at that point, she was pretty sure someone had been singing her praises.

'Well, that's worth hanging around for, don't you think?' said Florentina. 'He's casting; that much I know. Also, someone told me that he was having a few issues with his wife.'

'She's just had a baby,' said Judith.

'Mazel tov and all that jazz,' said Florentina. 'I'm just repeating what I was told. You're the one with your nipples out for inspection.'

Judith gave her a withering look. 'You want me to fix your bra too, don't ya?'

'You fucking know I do,' said Florentina, and they both laughed.

Alan Tomlinson was one of those directors that people had started talking about. He divided opinion. Some felt he was a visionary who could really do interesting work because he was

41

passionate and opinionated and charismatic. Others saw him as a well-educated do-gooder who was wasting his time in the regions because he couldn't make it in the West End. Depending on whether they'd been given a job or not, actors either declared him a leading force of the theatre, an 'actor's director', or an overrated artist with friends in high places.

The actors were gathered on the stage, some still in costume, others, somewhat miraculously, changed, showered and repainted. Veronica lingered at the back. She did want Alan to notice her but her status in the company was pretty low and she knew better than to stick her neck out and become unpopular and pushy on her first serious production.

Alan was brought onto the stage by their director, Claude, who introduced the principals and then stepped back to let Alan speak.

'I couldn't leave tonight without saying something,' said Alan.

Claude, who in other circumstances could have been annoyed at this showboating, was enjoying the association. His own reputation for drawing-room drama rep needed updating. He was acting like this young maverick was his new best friend.

Alan praised the cast, highlighted choice moments from the show and thanked everyone.

'I won't keep you a moment longer. You all need your rest I'm sure.'

Veronica moved off the stage with those who weren't lingering to speak to Alan.

'Well, thank you so very much Mr Tomlinson,' someone was muttering sarcastically. 'Do you think he was pissed off that Claude didn't curtsy?'

Two days later Veronica saw a letter in her pigeon-hole at the stage door. An envelope addressed but without a stamp and inside it a postcard. A painting of Ellen Terry on one side and a note on the other from Alan Tomlinson. He wrote that he found her fascinating. He had only come to the show the other night to see her and he was disappointed they hadn't had a chance to talk. He needed to see her again soon. He requested she respond, "with all convenient speed". He used quotation marks.

Veronica read the phrase out load where she stood. 'With all convenient speed.'

'*Merchant of Venice*,' the stage door man responded.

'Oh, yes. Thanks. Yes.' Veronica decided to pick up a copy from the second-hand bookshop between shows. She was smiling as she walked up the stairs to her dressing room. It was hard not to.

By the time Alan Tomlinson came to her flat she was edgy and slightly hilarious. She'd cleaned up but, more than that, she'd had a clear out. She'd tucked away the framed photo of herself as a little girl in tap shoes. It was a publicity shot from her first professional role, playing a dancing elf in a local panto. It was cute but rather silly. Veronica had also thrown away the magazines. She hadn't seen anyone backstage reading women's magazines and wasn't sure if that meant that it was something that serious actors didn't do. She shuffled the books so that the more impressive ones were centre stage. Earlier that day she had invested in a new poster – 'Water Lilies'. It looked good taped to the wall above the kitchen counter.

Her flat was a bedsit. One room in the attic of a large house with a bed and chest of drawers on one side, a kitchenette with stove, fridge and sink on the other. If you opened the door too wide you hit the settee that just fit into the space between the bed and the wall. She had a card table that she used to eat her meals. That was the only other piece of furniture in the room. For this occasion, Veronica had covered the table with a pretty cloth and positioned a pile of letters and the script of the play she was in on top to lend an air of spontaneity. The *mise en scène* of a young actress, broke but with potential, an artist at the start of an illustrious career.

When he arrived, Alan didn't look at anything but her. He was confident, striding up to her for a kiss and then flopping down on the settee as if he'd been there a hundred times. It made her want to laugh. She had intended to appear sophisticated, mysterious even, remind him of Leslie Caron in *The L-Shaped Room*, instead she had a huge grin and just nodded along to everything he was saying and tried really hard not to chuckle.

When he rolled and lit a cigarette, Veronica had to open a window to avoid any future complaints from her landlady. The old lady seemed to have a sixth sense about everything that went on in every bedsit. With the window open, the gas stove kept blowing out and Veronica was forced to stand by the cooker as the kettle bubbled, reigniting the flame every few moments until the water boiled. By the time she'd done it six times, she was laughing properly.

'I'm not a big tea drinker,' said Alan, laughing too.

'Good job, really. You could die of thirst this rate.'

Alan walked over to the kitchenette and, the next time Veronica leaned forward to hit the ignite button, put his arms around her. She leaned back into him and hugged his arms as he squeezed. His hands looked enormous in comparison to hers, smooth but with nails bitten and fingers and thumbs yellowed. Hers looked dainty, pale and pretty. The contrast was charming. She barely noticed his wedding ring.

Having an affair with Alan Tomlinson was impossible to keep secret. Despite Alan urging her to be very discreet, word got out backstage and Veronica had to admit to herself that she was glad that it had. People immediately started treating her differently. Florentina and Judith wanted an introduction to the director. They weren't shy about asking. Veronica promised to see what she could do but never did mention it to Alan.

She mostly saw him at her flat, although occasionally he met her in the greasy spoon around the corner from the theatre. Alan was in rehearsals himself and changed plans frequently when run-throughs ran over or he had unexpected meetings to attend. He would send a message round to the stage door, usually another white envelope with a postcard inside. Once he sent a record in a paper bag from Woolworths with a card that just said, 'see you on Sunday, my Juliet.' It was an LP of Peter, Paul & Mary. It was the first present he'd given her.

The next morning, before she was due at the theatre, Veronica popped in to her Mum's place to pick up her Dansette record-player.

Veronica's mother, also called Veronica, had retired from the factory where she had sewn gloves since she was a teenager but busied herself each day taking in sewing jobs. She had moved to a maisonette on the Batemoor Estate after her husband had died. The two Veronicas had lived there together for 18 months but it had not been easy. 'Our Veronica' (the younger) had been on the verge of leaving when her father passed away and had been pressured into staying to help 'Big Veronica' (the elder) to cope. Without the father's calming influence, the two women found too many reasons to argue and too few to get along. Eventually, as Our Veronica was approaching her 25th birthday, she had found the bedsit and made her escape. It was difficult to say if things were easier between them now they no longer lived together. Veronica made a point of seeing her mother a couple of times a month and called her weekly on Sunday at four o'clock before her mother's favourite TV programme, but they rarely talked about anything much, just updated each other on the facts of the week. Veronica still had a room in the maisonette and stayed there at Easter and Christmas. Her bicycle was still in the bedroom along with her now-empty fish tank and the Dansette.

'Can I borrow the trolley?' Veronica struggled as she carried the record-player down from her bedroom.

'You're not going to lug that thing all the way to the theatre and then home, are you?' said her mother, watching from the bottom of the stairs.

'Well, it'll be easier if I can borrow the trolley.'

'I'll need it back before weekend. You know I like to go to covered market when Brenda's there and she's got a half-day on fish this Saturday.'

'I'll get it back to you before the weekend, OK?' Veronica was strapping the red box, closed and taped shut, onto the wobbly black wheels.

'The road is like a bloody nightmare, council's done nothing, you just watch how you walk and keep those wheels straight.'

'Alright. See you, Mum.'

'Shall I get you a little piece of hake from Brenda when I see her?' said Big Veronica, but her daughter had already started down the street and the door closed shut by itself.

Most mornings Veronica would lie on her bed listening to the record and daydreaming about Alan. She could waste away hours like this, smiling to herself as the music washed over, so familiar now that she barely heard it. She imagined what it would be like when they lived together. She reran conversations they'd had and invented conversations they might have when she saw him next. She remembered what it felt like to be with him in her little flat. She liked the weight of him on her, pressing down so she felt breathless. She liked once their frantic need for each other was satisfied, that he would lie squashed between her and the cold wall, recklessly free of sheets and blankets which always ended up in a puddle at the end of the bed, both boldly naked, shameless. He would draw his finger along her arm and down her hip as if he was tracing her outline, making a copy for himself to take away when he left the flat and returned to his other life.

Being with Alan felt like being welcomed into a world that she'd always imagined but before now had no idea how to get to. He'd sit talking about what was really going on in a play or a film, how he saw something beyond the initial story, how the characters resonated in ways that most of the audience didn't see. He was an insider, an artist. And by association she was now too. She was different from the people she'd grown up with, rescued from the path they all trod that only went from school to work, from being a good girl to being a good wife, from duty to responsibility. With Alan, work didn't have to be about earning money, it could be about self-expression. The work an artist did could mean something. She knew that she was faking it somewhat during her conversations with him, that she wasn't so far away from the people she'd been at school with who shrugged off Shakespeare as boring and scoffed at the idea of classical music or wouldn't dream of paying to see a film with subtitles. But even faking it was better than being the young woman she would have been if she hadn't been able to sing.

There was no explanation for why Veronica could sing so well. People called it a gift and it often felt like one to Veronica, surprising and maybe something she didn't really deserve. She could sing and others in her school, in her neighbourhood, in her family couldn't. She'd been told for years that her voice was special. Knowing that made her ambitious. Once someone, then another, then many people told Veronica that her voice could take her places, she had allowed herself the pleasure of imagining those places. Where would she go and when? It hardly mattered as long as it wasn't here, with these people and their small lives. Alan loved her voice but he also loved her body. Veronica thought he might even love her too.

After a few months, their relationship became common knowledge and they started socialising together as a couple. Alan had left his wife. It was difficult, he said. He didn't give any details and Veronica didn't ask for any. One day he suggested she meet him at his theatre; she should come in to watch the rehearsal for his next show. He wanted her opinion. The auditorium was gloomy with houselights dimmed and the stage spot lit. A long table had been set up over the seats halfway up the stalls and behind it sat Alan and his assistant. The table was covered with papers, drawings, a cardboard model of the set design and a couple of overflowing ashtrays. For the next few hours, before Veronica had to swap theatres to be ready for her call, she watched Alan direct the actors, negotiate with the musicians and talk through his ideas with the stage manager and crew. Veronica was captivated. He was different from Claude in so many ways. He let the actors complete their scenes before stopping to share notes, he laughed along with the jokes, he rolled one cigarette after another until she could tell her own clothes were starting to stink of nicotine. He was cool. When the time came and she got up to leave, Alan pulled her towards him and kissed her on the lips in front of everyone. They were official.

Veronica left the theatre and hurried to catch the bus that would take her to The Playhouse. She was in a lovely half-dream as the bus chugged through the streets of Sheffield. It was only when she noticed the smell of the bloke sitting next to her that her reverie was interrupted. He stank. A stale body smell that made her feel sick. She held her scarf to her face and tried to breathe through her mouth, but the sick feeling didn't go away and the more she thought about it the more sick she felt. She'd had this sensation before. It was like she could smell everything in minutest detail. The man beside her, the discarded crisp packet on the floor, the scum in the ridge of the window... The hair of the old lady in the seat in front had a nauseating chemical pong. Yes, Veronica knew she was pregnant at that point. She recognised how her body worked and smell was the first warning sign. She decided that she wouldn't worry about it just yet. She'd see what happened. No need to rush straight around to Aunty Ruby's like the last time. That was totally different. That had been a complete and utter mistake after a one-night stand. This was just totally utterly different.

Veronica saw Alan two or three more times over the next ten days and each time she didn't get around to telling him. In fact, the first person Veronica ended up telling about her pregnancy was her mother, although she never would have planned it that way. She had agreed to stay the night at Batemore for her mum's birthday. They'd been to the Bernie Inn in the centre of Sheffield and had had a nice enough time, although things got frosty during the bus ride home.

'We could have cooked that meal ourselves for half the price,' said Big Veronica.

'That's not the point, is it?'

'Well, I don't know what the point is.'

'It's about the atmosphere, not having to cook it yourself. For God's sake, Mum, it's your birthday.'

'Oh, you know I don't like to make a fuss.'

'Well, you weren't happy when Alan took me away at Easter and I didn't come with you to Brenda's party.'

'I just don't see any good coming from you hanging out with a man like that.'

'A man like what?'

Even as her anger was tickling away inside and her mouth pinched into a scowl, Big Veronica wasn't likely to admit that her daughter was seeing a married to every nosey parker on the bus.

'You know exactly what I mean. The sooner you go and find someone suitable the better I'll sleep at night.'

'What? Now you're not sleeping at night?' said Veronica, 'And that's down to me and my gallivanting, I suppose?'

Her mother hushed her abruptly and stared out the window.

'I think it's probably a good idea for you to get used to Alan,' said Veronica. 'We're serious about each other, Mum.'

Her mother didn't unfix her eyes from the window. 'You say another bleeding word here on this bus and I'll have your guts for garters.'

Once inside the front door, the argument flared up quickly.

'You're a fancy woman for a married man and it's all I can do to walk out in the street without hanging my head in shame. Can you just imagine what they're all saying?'

'Mum, I don't care what they're saying. Why should I care? This is my life and nothing to do with anybody on the estate.'

'Of course, you don't care because I am the one living here, getting the looks, answering their questions, covering up for you.'

'Who's asking questions? What do you mean, questions?'

'You have made yourself the talk of the town.'

Suddenly, Veronica wanted to smile. The talk of the town – it seemed like something an actress should be aspiring to. She put her hand over her mouth, so no smirk would get through.

Her mother was silent for a moment, chewing her lips like she was summoning up the words she needed from deep in her gut. Veronica watched her mother's face contorting, as if in real physical pain. She took it all in and promised herself that she'd remember that expression, that mix between anger and agony on her mother's face, and perhaps use it on stage in future.

'Are you pregnant?' And that was it. It was out there. Veronica didn't respond directly but she told her mother that she was going to marry Alan. He was getting a divorce, and everything would be sorted before the baby was born.

Big Veronica was quiet. The reality of the situation hung in the air, uninvited, unwelcome and very real. Before her daughter left, Big Veronica took off the wedding ring she still wore.

'The least you can do is wear this from now on,' she said handing it over.

The next morning Veronica went into the theatre to see Alan. He was in his office and he was happy to see her.

'I'd like you to audition for the company,' he said. 'I've got a part in mind for you in A Doll's House. Small part but it would get you into the company and then I can think what I want to do with you.'

For Veronica this should have been an incredible moment, but she had to get to the point. There was no way round it.

'I'm pregnant,' she said, and Alan looked confused.

'Are you sure?' he said.

She didn't answer.

'OK,' he said. 'It'll be fine. This is going to take some jiggery pokery but it'll be fine. It's a period drama so you can be pretty well covered up.'

Veronica was sitting at Alan's desk as he walked around, talking as he paced.

'I'll have to leave Sarah,' he said. 'We'll get another place, I can't live at yours. It's probably worth you starting to look for somewhere that could work for us.'

Veronica hadn't taken her eyes off him and he glanced back at her and smiled weakly.

'Could work for us and the baby,' he said.

'I thought you had already left Sarah.'

'I have – I've been living there – you knew that, didn't you? I'll sort it out with her. Look, it's great. We'll sort everything out. I've got to go and see someone about something. I've got to see if I can catch the lighting guy before he goes. Wait here, I'll be back in a sec.'

As he reached the door, he turned and smiled. 'Oh, and you'll think about the audition, yeah?'

Once the door shut, the room was very quiet. Veronica swivelled around to face the desk and inspected the mess on top of it as she waited for Alan to return. She wasn't sure if that was a good reaction or a bad reaction. It wasn't quite the tears of joy that she might have fantasized about, but at least he was happy. He didn't seem to object to the idea of them starting a family.

In front of Veronica was a small cardboard model of the stage design for *A Doll's House*. No bigger than a cake box, the little stage had miniature cardboard furniture and paper people that stood on slivers of cork, with matchsticks to hold them straight. There was a little paper man in a green suit, a little paper woman in a fancy dress, a maid in a black uniform and two little paper children. Each was painted with the tiniest expressions, with smiles so delicate that they could have been painted with a single hair. The man had a moustache. The maid had glasses.

Veronica stared at the scene for a while. She wanted to touch the characters, to move them around, see them interact with each other. But she knew she shouldn't touch. It was delicate, and it was probably set up for a specific scene that Alan was working on.

Veronica waited a while for Alan. Eventually she decided to leave. She could see him later. She jotted a note on a pad on his desk. "Come and see me tonight, darling."

Lifting herself out of the chair, her eyes returned to the model stage. The paper woman had her arm up as if she was singing or crying out. Veronica leant across the desk and flicked her over.

She didn't get the part as the maid in *A Doll's House*, but she was asked to sing in an upcoming review. She'd be joining Alan's company for this show at least, and her career could finally take off. She told her mum and her friends and started working with the musical director. Veronica wanted to be great. She wanted to prove that she hadn't just been chosen because she was the girlfriend of the artistic director. She wasn't nervous so much as determined.

Veronica's body was swelling and everything she wore felt tight. Her shoes pinched and squeezed as she walked to work each day and by the time she undressed each evening her clothes had marked her body with red lines. But she sounded good. Her voice was strong and her own. Nobody sang like she did.

When the first night came, it was all a bit of a mess, the costume not quite fitting, people in and out of the dressing room, no time to go through the song in its entirety because the MD was running late. She was not in the calm frame of mind that she had hoped to be.

As it was a first night, the theatre was full. Veronica's song was opening the show and she stepped into place in the dark, behind the curtain, centre stage. She could hear some of the audience taking their seats, apologising to each other as they shuffled down the rows, chit-chatting as the house lights dimmed. Veronica looked to the side of the stage, but it was empty except for the manager who was bent over a cue board with a desk lamp illuminating the script in front of him. The band started, the curtain rose, the lights went up.

Within a bar, Veronica was flying. She avoided glances of people in the first few rows and sang out to the back, to the twinkling of glasses and blurred human shapes that made up the rest of the audience. They were all watching her. The blood that raced through her body was molten. *'I'll sing to him, each spring to him, and long for the day when I'll cling to him. Bewitched, bothered and bewildered... am I.'* Veronica heard a gasp from someone. She knew it was for her. She had made that happen. And they clapped. The warmth of that audience, more comforting than a hundred parents, more exhilarating than a thousand lovers... it was pure joy knowing that she had brought about that change in atmosphere. She had made people feel that.

She walked off stage past the actors standing ready to enter for the sketch that followed. 'Nice one,' said one of the fellas.

'Nice one,' she repeated to herself softly.

III

The baby came, and it was dramatic. So dramatic that Veronica forgot to analyse what she was going through so she could use it in her acting later. There was the surprise of her waters breaking while she was in the supermarket and the man behind the cold meats saying, 'Hey, love, you can't do that here.' There was the chaos as the manager called an ambulance and Veronica was crying and not remembering where she was supposed to be going or what she was supposed to do. There was the awkwardness when the nurse booked her in and made a point of saying 'Miss Gibson' even though she was there with other howling women who all probably had husbands in the waiting room pacing back and forth and smoking cigarettes like they do in films. For a while, Veronica felt that she might die. The doctor was business-like and practical. He had seen it all before, he said. She was no different from any other woman going through childbirth. It was what her body was made for, no need to fuss, just chomp down on this tube, suck in the gas and air and you'll have your baby in no time.

When the baby finally emerged, it was silent. The midwife told Veronica she'd had a daughter and took her over to the sink to wash off the goop.

'Can I see her?' Veronica asked.

'There'll be time enough for that,' said the midwife. 'You just focus on expelling the placenta. You'll feel contractions again soon.'

'Is she ok? She's not crying.'

'She's just fine. Seven pounds on the dot.'

When Veronica was finally back on the ward, in a clean gown, with her baby in her arms, Alan came in, with a bunch of flowers and a card signed by all the company at the theatre.

'They told me it was a daughter,' he said.

'Are you disappointed?' Veronica asked.

'No. Look at her. She's lovely. My darling, I'm so happy.'

Alan couldn't stay long. He left as soon as Big Veronica arrived, kissing the baby and Veronica and promising to return the next day. Alan leaned over to give Big Veronica a kiss and the older woman stuck out her cheek stiffly so that they connected with the hospital bed between them.

'Thanks for coming, Mum,' Veronica said once Alan had left and Big Veronica had pulled up a chair.

'Well, she's my granddaughter. I'm not going to miss this. And what a lovely little thing. She looks like…' She paused and studied the crimson baby head, which was all that was available to inspect of the swaddled child.

'I know, Mum, she looks like a potato.'

'All babies look like potatoes,' Big Veronica smiled. 'But she also looks like you.'

Years later, after Natalie herself had had her first child, Veronica would say that Natalie revealed her personality in those first few days in hospital. Her calm confidence, her way of watching the world, assessing things before making any decision.

'You were like an adult in a baby's body,' Veronica would say.

But in truth, neither Natalie nor Veronica felt comfortable in the world they found themselves in at that time. Both were happier when the nurse was there to tuck in the blanket, flip the little person over her shoulder and pat her on the back until a gravelly pop issued forth. When the nurse left mother and baby to it, the new mother was awkward, the baby unsettled. Veronica held the baby stiffly like a doll that shouldn't be played with. Natalie flopped in her arms, her unfocussed eyes wide and her face in a frown that already looked judgemental.

Veronica waited for the surge of love that she'd been promised. She knew from friends she'd spoken to that the warm glow of love for your child after its birth could not be equalled. However, the warm glow didn't come as expected. Instead, Veronica felt miscast. She kept it very quiet but had to admit, if only to herself, that if someone had offered to take the baby away for a few months and return it once it was a little more robust and able to communicate what it wanted, Veronica would have been very happy.

Alan drove them back from the hospital to the cottage they had rented on the edge of the moors. It was foggy outside, and the car was filling up with smoke from Alan's cigarette, so the whole journey was driven through a blur. Veronica sat with Natalie in her arms in the passenger's seat, full of trepidation about what she'd do when they got home and the baby woke up. Alan was quiet too. Although not quite a married couple – that would come in a few weeks time – Veronica already knew Alan well enough to recognise that when he was quiet he was rarely thinking about what was going on around him and more than likely in a completely different scenario, usually one that related to the next play or the current play or a play that he'd not even read yet.

The house had been decorated with a banner that said 'Welcome Home Baby'. Although Veronica could sense that the effort had been made by someone on the theatre staff, and the flowers arranged in a vase on the kitchen table without a card had probably been placed there by Alan's secretary, she was chuffed that he'd gone to the trouble of asking for that to be done and she certainly wasn't going to ruin the moment when she could just go along with the scene as it appeared.

'How sweet of you, my darling,' she said, placing their little daughter in a carry cot that had been left in front of the Aga.

'She likes it,' Alan said, coming over to hug the mother of his child. For a few minutes the two of them stood looking down into the box which held their sleeping baby.

Eventually Veronica said, 'I should get us some dinner.'

'Don't worry my love,' Alan dropped his arm from around Veronica's waist now the spell was broken. 'I'm going to the theatre later and I'll get a snack there.'

'Tonight, you're going out?' Veronica tried to downplay her disappointment.

'Bruce is understudying tonight, and I want to see him,' he said. He could tell that Veronica was surprised. 'He's your friend and I gave him a chance, but I need to see him in front of an audience.'

'Of course,' she said, 'but you didn't give Bruce the job just to make me happy, did you? I wouldn't want...'

'I would do anything for you,' Alan said and swooped forward to dance with her. He put his arms around Veronica again and left them there, swaying to the silent music. 'No, I gave him a chance because he's good, could be right for *Caucasian Chalk Circle*. You'll be fine here, won't you? I wouldn't go unless you were going to be OK.'

'I'm going to be OK,' said Veronica. At that moment the baby woke and started coughing and crying in alternate gasps.

'My cue,' she said.

'And mine,' said Alan, stepping back from the carry cot and moving towards his coat.

Veronica stayed where she was in the kitchen and fed the baby. Alan kissed her sweetly and promised he'd only watch the first act and then return.

She looked at the door for a while once he'd closed it behind him. Their cottage was freshly painted and neither Alan nor Veronica had had time to put up any pictures or do much more than move the furniture in. Veronica looked at the walls, counted the marks and lumps that should have been fixed before the paint went on. The baby continued to feed.

The house was quiet and now that she was sitting on her own, a long distance from the city, she realised how much company she had inadvertently enjoyed from her neighbours in the bedsit. The man next door calling for his cat, the old dear downstairs with the wireless up too loud. Here she was alone. It felt a new experience and not a good one. Only a few weeks before she'd been on stage, held up by the affection of the audience, hundreds of people all with her, looking at her, smiling too, a real connection. You could never be lonely up there on stage with all that attention pouring over you.

'Just me and you tonight, little one,' she said to the baby who had detached from her breast and was dozing with mouth open and eyes only half closed. As she watched little Natalie snooze, Veronica started to sing softly. 'Me and my shadow / Strolling down the avenue, / Me and my shadow, / Not a soul to tell our troubles to... And when it's twelve o'clock, / We climb the stair, / We never knock, / For nobody's there...'

Eight weeks later, an au pair had been found and Veronica was ready to join the read through of *The Caucasian Chalk Circle*. The au pair, a grand title for a local girl called Audrey who had done some baby-sitting but never lived in with a family before, was given a room at the back of the house with French doors to the garden. It was the nicest room in the house, but Veronica was happy for her to have it. The fact that the garden backed onto the moors spooked Veronica and she was more comfortable sleeping upstairs. Audrey was a quiet girl, chunky and badly-dressed. She was the type of girl who chewed on her hair and rarely made eye contact. It came as a surprise to both Alan and Veronica when later they learned that she had been welcoming local boys in through the French doors while they were at work. Despite her lack of experience, Audrey was good with the baby, and the steady stream of young men who hopped over the garden fence during the eight shows a week didn't distract her from her duties. Veronica felt more relaxed and enjoyed waking up to the sound of Audrey playing peek-a-boo with Natalie downstairs.

The read-through started at noon. A rehearsal room had been set out for the occasion with tables forming a large square in the middle. As the actors arrived they chatted and took their seats. Although Veronica and Alan had driven in together from home, Veronica asked if she could enter the rehearsal room before him. It bothered her that she would be seen as the director's wife rather than as an actor in her own right. Despite Alan lingering in the corridor smoking for a few minutes to accommodate her, the actors and assistant director were engrossed in noisy conversations and most didn't notice the effort that had been made by the two of them to arrive independently.

Veronica's friend Bruce had been cast and was bubbling with excitement, telling jokes and leaning across the table, stretching his hand out to introduce himself to anyone who might not have met him before. Veronica went and sat beside him.

'Great to see you, Vee,' he said, swinging his arm around her. 'How's the nipper?'

'She's great. She loves Audrey. It's all worked out really well. I'm just so lucky to have found someone who could start straight away and was happy to live in.'

'And the fact that she looks like the side of a house is a bonus I suppose?'

'What do you mean by that?' Veronica said, frowning, but the rehearsal was starting, and Alan was calling for everyone's attention. Bruce turned his chair to face his director, cutting her off.

'This play has never been more relevant,' Alan was saying. It was a version of the speech that he'd given to the administrators, based on a version he had given to the Arts Council. Veronica had discussed the play with him before both of those meetings. She smiled as he incorporated a couple of points she had suggested. Here she was in a serious play, with her serious new husband and even her best friend in the cast. For a split second she thought of Natalie back at home in the cottage and her breasts ached. She'd use that. A mother's unbreakable bond to her child. The deep love that made them human and could illicit a passion deeper than any other. Oh yes, she'd use that.

Working with Alan was the best way to stay close to him, Veronica realised over the weeks as the play took shape. He confided in her and consulted her about a variety of things quite openly in front of the other members of the cast. He made it clear that her opinion was respected. They gave up putting on a show of arriving or leaving separately. Instead Veronica would wait for him until the end of each day, whether she was needed or not, and they'd drive home together chatting about the day or just sitting in silence and enjoying each other's company.

'Did you have this kind of relationship with Sarah?' Veronica asked and instantly regretted it. She wished she could take the words back immediately. Bringing up Alan's ex-wife was inviting her into the car with them and Veronica didn't even want to know the answer. It was like she was giving Alan a test and she didn't want him to pass or fail it. Maybe she should change the subject?

'It was a volatile relationship,' Alan said, using the same voice that he did when discussing character. He didn't seem upset with the subject and Veronica was enormously relieved. 'The whole experience brought out the worst in both of us. You and she are very different but it's actually possible that you could have been friends.'

'Oh.' Veronica still wanted to talk about something else. She didn't need any detail; she just wanted to know that he was happier now than he had been, and that was enough. Only wanted to feel secure that she was the woman that made him happy.

'Sarah was with me when I was just starting out,' he continued. 'She was... she is organised... practical. She's very accomplished. Can put her mind to anything. It was great to be involved with someone like that.'

'Yes, I can imagine,' said Veronica, trying to be warm but

doubting she was convincing.

'I needed her. I think she needed me too. Then she had the baby. We both needed each other less.'

Veronica bit her tongue hoping that was the end of the conversation.

'When I met you, I realised what I had been missing. You are an artist.'

And there it was. The validation. Just what she needed to assure her that the game had been won, that there could be no rivalry between the current and former Mrs Tomlinson, because a decision had been made. The words would sustain her for weeks to follow. She would bring them to mind when Alan was off in London at meetings and she was alone. They would comfort her when he went to see his son for the afternoon and left her with Natalie and the au pair. And, despite the initial fear that her career would never move ahead like it should, they would be her mantra when she found out that she was pregnant again two months later.

Veronica's second pregnancy couldn't have been more different from the first. As an actress married to the director of the city's Lyceum Theatre, the news made the local papers. She didn't have to hide the fact that she was expecting and enjoyed the fuss from colleagues and letters and gifts that some of the fans dropped around to the theatre. An interview with her appeared in *The Sheffield Herald* with a photo of her and Natalie at their cosy cottage. Veronica spoke enthusiastically about her plans to stay acting, to stay in Sheffield and to stay in the house by the moors. There could be no better place to bring up a family. As Alan had been away at the time, the photographer couldn't get a photo of the three of them together, so the paper printed a separate picture of Alan to accompany the article. Veronica was miffed that the one they used showed Alan with his '50s glasses and beatnik polo neck sweater rather than as he looked now with longer hair and sexy sideburns. The photo had been taken when he was married to Sarah. Veronica wondered if Sarah would see the article and what her reaction would be.

Big Veronica was elated. She was able to hold her head high on the estate and she started a scrapbook just for stories of the growing family. Big Veronica could get free tickets to see any of the shows she wanted, and she came to the theatre often with her friend, Brenda. Both of them would make a day of it, coming into the city centre early to get their hair fixed into gravity-defying beehives and grabbing a bite to eat and a cuppa in the theatre caff before seeing the show. They preferred a musical but sat through everything from *The Merchant of Venice* to *The Resistible Rise of Arturo Ui* without complaint, always saying 'that's not something I'm ever likely to forget' to the actors in the dressing room afterwards.

Veronica hadn't stayed at her mother's maisonette in Batemoor since Natalie had been born. But the two Veronicas did see each other weekly now and there was less tension between them. Sunday lunch became a bit of a tradition with Big Veronica arriving on Sunday morning with something tasty from the market. She'd kiss her granddaughter, chastise Audrey for spoiling the baby or dressing her in the wrong clothes for the weather they were having, and then she'd start cooking. Her own daughter, the actress on her one day off, would lay in bed with her husband until lunch was ready. Sometimes Alan and Veronica would ask a friend or two over. Bruce came at least once a month. Big Veronica loved it when there was an additional guest, especially when it was her daughter's best pal. Bruce had just the right level of enthusiasm for the food prepared as well as entertaining stories that kept them laughing through to the apple crumble. Once in a while, when he wasn't going out that evening, Bruce even drove Big Veronica home to Batemoor.

'When are you going to find yourself a nice young lady?' she would ask when they were alone together in the car on the way home.

'Don't go holding your breath on that one, Big Vee,' he'd say.

Christmas panto time came and Veronica was cast as the wicked fairy, with a costume resembling a large black dandelion to hide her body's changing shape. She didn't realise that she was stepping into controversy by taking on a role that in the past had always gone to one of the older members of the company. Lizzie Bell had been 'part of the furniture' for decades and, even though she was no longer cast in many of the plays being put on in repertory, she was expected to be seen in the role of a bad fairy or nasty queen each year for the panto. Alan had decided that the time had come for a change. Despite an awkward call from Lizzie's Bell's agent, a word of warning from the company manager and some whispered comments from other cast members, he had cast his own wife in the role and refused to justify his decision.

Rehearsals moved ahead without incident, but the first night review came down hard on the show and in particular its director and his wife. Alan was accused of nepotism and showing a lack of respect for tradition. Worse, Veronica was reported to be a less than suitable replacement for the beloved old girl of the Sheffield theatre scene. 'Instantly forgettable and without the personality to carry off a comic role.' Veronica was shaken. Alan was livid.

'It's nothing to do with your performance,' he assured her. 'Please don't let it get to you.'

The following afternoon Alan dropped Veronica off at the theatre early. Veronica had two shows that day, like most days during panto season; he had a meeting so left her at the stage door. She felt self-conscious about going into work after the appalling review, but Bruce was waiting to console her and joke around as she got ready.

After the show, Bruce offered to drive her home and came in for a glass of wine. Natalie and Audrey were long asleep, but Alan was sitting in the lounge reading and listening to *The Mothers of Invention*.

'Good show?' he asked.

'Great,' said Bruce. 'We had a couple of coachloads of old

folks laughing themselves silly.'

'We're having wine, do you want a glass?' called Veronica from the kitchen.

'How was she today?' Alan asked Bruce under his breath. 'That shitty review could have thrown her.'

'All good,' said Bruce. 'Nobody mentioned it. I think she realises that that journalist was just picking at the show because Lizzie Bell is probably a friend of his.'

'The guy's a dick,' Alan said. 'I went in to see him today and he almost shat himself. He was not expecting that.'

'What did you say? What did he say?'

'Hey, we've both got our jobs to do. I actually went in to give him tickets for the preview of *Duchess of Malfi*. But you should have seen his face when I walked through the door.'

Veronica arrived back with a bottle of wine and three glasses.

'Not for me, darling,' said Alan getting up. 'I'm done in. Night night you two.' He kissed Veronica and gave Bruce a wave as he went upstairs.

'I need this,' Veronica said, pouring herself a large glass.

Bruce was quiet for a while, listening to the record and sipping his wine. Then he couldn't hold it in any longer. He pulled his chair up closer to Veronica and leaned towards her conspiratorially.

'Do you know that Alan went to see that journalist today?'

'What? No?'

'The hack that wrote the review about the panto.'

'He did? My God, what happened?'

'Well, seems like he put the wind up the guy. That's for sure.'

Veronica smiled.

Bruce stayed the night on the sofa and the next day he convinced Veronica to come to church with him. Bruce was doing a Bible reading and he wanted some moral support from his friend.

'Those old birds in the church are harsh critics. They expect the right amount of piety or they complain to the priest.'

Veronica hadn't been to church for a long time and sat with

Bruce in a pew towards the front. The church was a modern building, with dramatic white walls that stretched up to form a pyramid above the parishioners. There was a stained-glass window above the door but no other religious paintings. It was pared down, elegant, very different from the churches Veronica had gone to with her mum or with school. This one could have been an art gallery or museum. It was futuristic. The streamlined chic was only marred by a paper flyer that had been taped up by the door, slightly skew-whiff, with a reminder of the bring-and-buy sale that was taking place the following weekend. The young vicar was enthusiastically welcoming the congregation and helping some of the older folks into the pews. He looked over to Bruce and smiled.

'He seems to like you,' whispered Veronica.

'We've had our moments,' said Bruce.

The service began with a hymn, and Bruce and Veronica were not shy about belting out a descant on the last verse. There were some prayers, then Bruce got up to read. It was a long passage and Veronica lost interest after a while, staring at the altar instead of watching Bruce in the pulpit and studying the crucifix behind it. Jesus was hanging there, as anticipated, but he was looking straight ahead rather than facing down, and his hands didn't seem to be hammered into place just held out against the wooden cross. It was more like he was reaching out for a bear hug.

Veronica thought of Alan. Her husband had taken her side and gone to see the journalist who had written that bad review. It made her feel warm. She had someone who was prepared to look out for her, to make sure she was safe, to wrap her up in his arms and keep all the bad stuff away. She trusted him. Alan was a great artist and she knew that if he had chosen her as his wife she must have something to offer. She must have talent herself. Veronica had always felt one step from disaster, one second from being exposed as just another uneducated over-confident loudmouth. She had survived until this point with luck, yet this nagging insecurity was something that she held in the back of her mind every day, like a subtle toothache. Now she had Alan. He would lead the way from here. He'd make sure their family was safe and happy. He could generate work for the both of them and take on any outsider that threatened them. Veronica screwed her face into a triumphant grin. She had everything she needed.

Bruce finished his reading and dropped his head down in a half-bow, half prayer. It took all Veronica's self-control not to applaud.

IV

Veronica and Alan's second daughter, Alice, was born on a Sunday. For the dedicated theatre couple, this was great timing and many of their friends remarked upon it in congratulatory cards, joking that her parents were both expected back at work for the following week's eight shows.

Veronica missed Bruce who was now in London with a new job and an agent who was known for helping actors get work in West End musicals. She was happy for Bruce and only a little jealous. She relied more and more on her other good friend, Bobbi, who had started coming to the weekly Sunday lunches. Although she'd never been to San Francisco, or even the United States, Bobbi was a flower child. She tied her long hair in colourful scarves and weighed herself down with strings of amber beads around her neck and leather wristbands and jangly bracelets up and down both arms. Bobbi could read the future by tuning into a person's aura. She would look deeply into a person's eyes, assess the glow that she said she could see emanating from their body and tell them some of the important things that were coming their way. Bobbi insisted it was easier to pick up the vibes after smoking hash and usually started her future-gazing ritual by warming a bit of the brown resin, rolling it between finger and thumb for a few minutes as she watched her subject closely. Then she'd lay out tobacco on a cigarette paper, add the sliver of hash, roll it, light it and sit back to share her thoughts.

When she met the new baby, Alice, Bobbi decided to see what she could do to predict the little girl's life ahead.

'Her aura is yellow,' she said after a few minutes staring at the sleeping child.

'Is that good?' said Veronica, who was taking this unexpectedly seriously despite initially scoffing at the idea.

'Yellow is positive,' said Bobbi. 'She'll be happy.'

'That's good.'

'I think she's going to have lots of adventures,' Bobbi announced.

'I hope so,' said Veronica.

'She's going to travel. She's going to see the world.'

For a while, the two women were quiet, watching the baby sleep. Bobbi's cigarette went out and she relit it, passing it to Veronica, who took a few puffs before handing it back.

'Have you ever looked at your own aura?' Veronica asked.

'No, I can't see my future,' Bobbi said.

'That's probably a good thing,' Veronica responded. 'If we knew what was going to happen, it might take away our motivation.'

As well as an amateur fortune-teller, Bobbi was a costume designer and had worked on many of Alan's productions. Yet she never seemed very keen to get back to work, unlike Veronica who felt panicky when she didn't know if she had a part in an upcoming production. Veronica still wasn't on a full contract with the company and felt the sting of unemployment after every show ended its run.

'Alan's talking about doing *The Cherry Orchard*,' Veronica said. 'I haven't spoken to him about whether there's a role for me. It's his decision, of course, but I thought I might mention that I'm keen. I can't just stay here, out in the middle of nowhere. I'll go mad. Do you want me to ask him about who's doing the costumes?'

'Nah. I'm not really looking to work at the moment. I'm just enjoying, you know, life around me.' Bobbi reached over and picked up Alice who had woken up. 'I love them when they're weeny like this.' The baby snuggled her face into Bobbi's neck.

'Yes, I know what you mean,' said Veronica. She was looking for the right word to sum up the affection she felt she should declare for her new baby. Alice, in Bobbi's arms, was now staring up into the sky, her eyes slightly crossed, her cheeks speckled with milk-spots and her hair slicked down as if Brylcreemed. 'Precious,' Veronica said eventually.

Alan gave Veronica a couple of weeks notice that his mother was coming to visit and was going to bring Alan's and Sarah's son, John. It still didn't feel like enough time to prepare. Veronica had met Alan's mother only a handful of times and had never spent enough time with her to form any kind of bond. Alan's mother was from London; she was academic and opinionated and insisted on being addressed as Bunny, which Veronica found awkward. She'd never met anyone called Bunny and certainly not a grown woman. Bunny was about as different from Veronica's mother as a woman could be. Where Big Veronica was practical and cautious, always aware of who might be judging her and her daughter and bending over backwards to fit into the background, Bunny spoke loudly, asked uncomfortable questions and shared her views with delight, especially if they contradicted those already expressed in the room. Veronica couldn't get a handle on whether Bunny approved of her marriage to Alan or not. Bunny had only visited their house in Sheffield twice, after both of their daughters had been born. Now she was coming for a third time and making a detour on her trip from London to pick up Alan's firstborn who was six years old but still a stranger to Veronica, Natalie and Alice.

If Veronica found the prospect of a visit from Bunny unsettling, Big Veronica found it fraught with danger. She volunteered to come and cook a suitable meal and help with the girls. She then changed her mind and said it would probably be better if she wasn't there to get under foot and potentially say the wrong thing. She flip-flopped over the decision for two weeks and eventually settled on helping with the cooking and cleaning before the special guests arrived, then making an exit an hour or two before they showed up.

As it happened, Bunny and John were late. The food was cold, and the little girls were both asleep by the time they arrived.

'He was too hungry to wait so we stopped at a transport café, didn't we?' Bunny leaned down to take off John's coat.

'I can do it, Granny,' said John. 'And it wasn't actually a transport café, it was a chain restaurant.'

Bunny laughed. 'There are no flies on this young man,' she said.

Alan hugged his son and held on to him as he ushered him into their living room where they had some presents laid out.

'Thank you very much,' the little boy said. 'I like colouring books a lot.'

'Can I get you something to drink?' asked Veronica, gathering the coats.

'No thank you,' said the boy. 'I'm quite full now.'

'A glass of sherry for me if you have it,' said Bunny, lowering herself onto the sofa. 'And here's where I'll stay,' she said. 'This is the perfect spot, just by the fire, with a view of the countryside. Perfect. I don't think I'll move for the next four days.'

Alan went to the kitchen to get the sherry, Veronica followed him in.

'She's staying for four days?' she asked.

They snacked on food in the lounge and sipped sherry until it was time for John to go to bed.

'I've brought a book for you to read to me,' he said getting up and going over to a small suitcase that he'd brought with him. 'I can read myself, of course, but it helps me to sleep if someone else does.'

'Perhaps I can read to you?' volunteered Veronica. 'It'll give your Granny and your Daddy a chance to catch up with each other.'

'That's very kind of you,' said the lad, 'but I'd sooner have

Dad read to me. As I don't know you yet it might make me a bit frightened to go to sleep here if you're the one reading the story.'

Alan stood up and walked over to the boy. 'Come along, young fellow,' he said, with his hand on his son's shoulder.

The boy walked solemnly to kiss his grandmother and his step-mother.

'Night night,' Veronica smiled. 'We'll have some fun tomorrow.'

When the boy had been taken upstairs and the sherry glasses refilled, the two women sat smiling at each other, waiting for the conversation to take off again.

'I usually like to sleep late but don't worry about the babies disturbing me,' Bunny said. 'I'll just take out my hearing aids and there can be murders and I'd be none the wiser. So, bring me up to speed, how old are the babies now and how is Alan coping living out here in the back of beyond?'

'Natalie is almost two, she's walking and talking, like a champ. She's going to start ballet in a couple of weeks; you'll not believe how sweet her little costume is. Alice is three months. She's a great baby. The most relaxed little thing, barely cries. It's amazing to see how they're both so different already. Natalie is strong-willed, you can see she's never going to be shy, she knows what she wants and will tell anyone. And Alice is a big smiley ball of loveliness. I can't wait for them to meet John. I've told them about their big brother and they're excited to show him their room.'

Veronica stopped talking as she realised that Bunny's eyelids had closed. She stayed quiet for a bit until she heard her mother-in-law's breathing get heavier and knew that she was definitely asleep. Veronica picked up the sherry glasses, the half-empty bottle and half-full ashtray, and carried them through to the kitchen.

Alan's son got on well with his half-sister Natalie and posed dutifully the next morning for a photo holding baby Alice. It was a beautiful day so they all sat in the garden with the baby in the shade of an umbrella and the two other kids running in and out of the house and enjoying each other's company.

After 20 minutes, Alan said he had some reading to do and he'd be upstairs.

'If I don't come down before lunch, come and wake me,' he said.

'I thought you said you are reading, or are you napping?' Veronica said, not thrilled that she was being left alone to entertain John and Bunny.

'An hour, max,' Alan said, laughing as if she'd made a joke.

'It's lovely to see the children playing together so nicely,' Veronica said after a few minutes of awkward silence.

'John gets on with everyone,' said Bunny. 'He's a credit to his parents.'

Veronica felt uncomfortable but thought it was highly likely she was reading insults into everything Bunny was saying. It was a habit she'd picked up from her own mother.

Bunny was watching her grandson with a look of pride. 'I said to his mother, to bring up a boy properly you need to tell him he's a genius – every day if you can. Tell him, he's superior.'

'John certainly does seem mature for his age.'

'He's self-assured. All the luck in the world can't help if you don't have that. I told Alan he was a genius until he believed it, and I intend to do the same with John.'

'Well, that's a bit of a contrast to how I was brought up,' said Veronica with a half-laugh.

'It's completely different for girls,' said Bunny. 'I knew that Alan could achieve great things.'

'And he has,' said Veronica.

'You will too,' Bunny responded.

This possible complement came so out of the blue, after such a frosty morning with her mother-in-law, that Veronica got tears in her eyes.

'Thank you,' she said.

'You just stay with Alan. Don't get in his way but cling

onto those coat-tails. As long as you don't stop him, nothing's stopping you.'

Before Veronica had time to question this, her step-son came running outside yelling.

'That little monster has ruined my crayons,' John said, rushing up to his grandmother and putting his head in her lap.

'What on earth is going on?' said Bunny angrily.

Veronica looked over to the house and saw Natalie in the doorway with her hands stained in rainbow colours and even some blue and purple around her lips.

'She's smushed everything,' John wailed.

'That's completely unacceptable,' said Bunny. 'Didn't she realise that she wasn't supposed to play with them?'

'She's a baby,' said Veronica getting up to go over to Natalie, who was crying now too.

'Now now,' Bunny soothed John, 'we can get you some more. Be a big boy, now.'

When things had calmed down, Natalie had been washed clean, John had been bribed into forgiveness by the offer of felt-tip pens and Bunny had started on a little glass of sherry to settle her nerves, Alan reappeared.

'An intriguing new play,' he said, dropping a script onto the table. 'I'd love you both to read it. I'm thinking of putting it into the next season.'

Veronica and Bunny looked at him.

'Didn't you hear the ruckus?' said Bunny. 'It's been like world war three down here.'

'Didn't hear a peep,' said Alan, 'I had headphones on.'

Each hour that Veronica spent in Bunny's company felt like five and by the time she could finally go to bed each night, she was exhausted. It was difficult to talk to Alan about his mother's veiled putdowns which, when repeated, didn't sound that bad, or her demanding ways or her non-interest in their daughters. Alan would laugh it off by saying 'She's quite a character', and Veronica didn't want to start a fight. She kept herself sane by counting the days until Bunny was leaving.

John was easier to get along with. He was unlike any six-year-old she'd ever met – a boy so used to spending time with adults that he felt comfortable in conversations, and Veronica enjoyed her chats with him as they took walks on the moors. He even helped put his half-sisters to bed, and she was charmed by his tenderness towards them. Once the crayon-eating incident was behind them, he became confident in the role of elder brother and even began to offer Veronica advice which she found endearing.

'I always have a glass of water by my bed,' he said one night as he helped her tuck in Natalie. 'I don't usually drink it but it's good to know it's there and I don't have to worry Mummy in the middle of the night. Maybe Natalie would like a little glass of water too.'

The night before Bunny and John were due to leave, Veronica invited her own mother for dinner, cooked a roast and put two bottles of white wine in the fridge. The light at the end of the tunnel was drawing closer and they'd soon have the house back to themselves.

Veronica's mother was early, ringing the doorbell although she had a key. Veronica opened the door and couldn't hide her surprise at her mother's appearance. Big Veronica had gone to an enormous effort to impress, including having her hair styled into a sky-scraper-high 'do', attaching false eyelashes and fastening her friend's fox wrap over her best green suit. The fur stole, which had the poor creature's head still attached, and beady glass eyes, gave the impression of an angry fox biting its own tail. It emitted an unmistakeable smell of mothballs.

'Good to see you, Ma,' said Veronica, hugging her. 'You look nice.'

Veronica, Alan and the kids were in the lounge with Big Veronica by the time Bunny made an entrance, and she did make an entrance, sweeping into the room and striding over to Big Veronica with her hand outstretched. Big Veronica couldn't conceal her alarm at being caught sitting on the floor with her grand-daughter in her lap, and Veronica noticed her mother glancing over at the fox stole that was hanging over the arm of the sofa as if for a moment she was wondering if she should put it on again.

'So lovely to see you again, Veronica,' said Bunny continuing her path towards her. Big Veronica looked around for somewhere to put baby Alice; then, sensing urgency because Bunny had finally arrived in front of her, she tucked the baby under her arm and knelt, reaching out a hand in greeting. The image of the two women shaking hands, one on her knees and the other bending in a half-bow, was something Veronica would always remember with embarrassment. It was the epitome of trying too hard. She knew exactly how her mother was feeling because she'd been feeling the same way for days.

Alan was talkative over dinner; wine flowed, and Bunny laughed loudly. The two Veronicas exchanged glances occasionally and both eventually settled down, realising that the evening was going pretty well. The meal arrived on the table steaming hot and tasty. The two youngest kids went to bed between courses and didn't cause a fuss, and little John amused everyone with stories about what he most liked about Yorkshire and what he'd tell his friends back in Oxford.

'Mummy would like it here too,' he said, and Veronica felt a stab of awkwardness returning, but her own mother replied,

'I'm sure she would, there's lots to see and do.' And the conversation continued.

When it came time for John to go to bed, he asked his new step-mother to read him a story. Veronica was touched and left her mother and Alan to organise coffee and open another bottle of wine.

John had been sleeping in a camp bed on the landing and, as Veronica read him a tale about Robin Hood, she could hear the murmur of voices from the kitchen below.

'Thanks for letting me stay,' said John yawning as she closed the book. 'I've really had a great time.'

'You're very welcome, John,' she replied. 'Any time.'

Before heading downstairs, Veronica peeked into the girls' room. Alice was asleep and still. Natalie too was gone for the count, her head hanging almost off the bed. Veronica went to rearrange her daughter and gave them both a kiss. She smiled as she tiptoed out of the room and passed the sleeping John. Theirs was an unusual family, perhaps, but the kids were happy there was no doubt.

As she made her way down the steps she heard Bunny's voice.

'We're all adults here,' she was saying. 'I don't see why this is such a difficult question for you, Veronica.'

Her heart sank. When she turned the corner to the kitchen, she saw her mother's face was white. She looked over to her daughter despairingly.

'Have you all had enough coffee?' Veronica said, hoping to change the subject from whatever agony she'd stepped into. 'While I'm up, I can put the kettle on again.'

'If you've got any more of that lovely sherry, I'll have a thimbleful,' said Bunny.

'Yes, me too,' said Alan.

Veronica walked around the table pouring a little glass for each of them. She touched her mother on the shoulder as she moved passed her.

'I think the current generation of young people just don't seem to understand that the sexual revolution started with us,' Bunny continued. The sherry had only acted as an intermission rather than a conclusion. 'As I was trying to get your mother to agree, Veronica, we all had numerous lovers before getting married and there were ways of solving little problems if they occurred.' She held the two fingers of each hand up in the air, miming quotation marks, on the word "problems". 'Of course, some of you, even in this day and age, decide to move ahead and have all the children you can pop out but, in my day, we were sensible. Well, if you had any sort of education or breeding you knew how to resolve any issues – that was unless you were poor or Catholic or something.'

The doorbell rang. Everyone looked startled or perhaps relieved. Veronica leapt up.

'Not expecting anyone, are we?' said Alan, reaching over to the bottle to refill his own glass and his mother's.

Veronica opened the door to Bobbi. In a long flowing dress, obviously without a bra, a scarf wrapped around her head, Bobbi entered, holding a tall stick, like a shepherd's crook.

'Sorry I was passing, and I promised Alan I'd drop this off.' She walked from the front door to the kitchen, using the staff as an elaborate walking-stick.

Alan stood as she entered.

'Hello, darling,' he said. 'Oh, is that the staff? Yes, it's perfect.'

Bunny coughed, chastising her son, who picked up quickly on the hint.

'Bobbi, this is my mother, Bunny. Mum, this is Bobbi who has worked with us at the theatre in costume and props.'

'And can I ask what you've come as?' Bunny leaned back in her chair, better to look down her nose at the intrusive visitor.

'Excuse me?' said Bobbi.

'Is that your regular ensemble, or are you dressed for a mardi gras?'

The two Veronicas were alarmed and held their breath as they watched the interaction.

Bobbi did a twirl. The dress flared out around her and her bangles jingled.

'Do you like it?' She giggled.

'In all seriousness, I can't imagine any type of situation where one would wear that,' said Bunny. 'You look like a wood nymph.'

'How nice of you to notice,' Bobbi handed over the stick to Alan. 'I can't come over to the theatre this week, but I know you wanted to copy this.'

She waved at the two Veronicas and swept towards the door. 'Sorry I can't stay – there's no rest for wood nymphs, you know. Ciao and cheerio.'

With Bobbi gone, Bunny huffed, 'That was a bit rude,

dropping around so late. Is she a friend of yours, Alan?'

Veronica stood to clear away the dinner at last. 'She's my friend,' she said emphatically. 'She's probably my best friend.'

With Bunny and John returned to their own homes, and Audrey back from the mini-holiday she'd been given, Veronica's spirits rose. She had a call from her agent with an interview booked in London. She'd need to go down for the day and decided to stay the night with Bruce who had promised she could kip on his sofa whenever she needed to. Following a week of preparations, a quick visit to her vocal coach to refresh her accent and make sure the Yorkshire vowels were under control, she kissed her babies goodbye, handed them over to Audrey and left.

Alan had been supportive of the idea of her going, which she appreciated, although as he waved her off at the station, she did wonder if he seemed a little too cheery to be getting rid of her for two whole days. A more heartfelt farewell would have been nice, but perhaps a Celia Johnson/Trevor Howard-style moment was too much to expect. Alan and she were both busy, and they were a married couple now. They could get away with taking each other for granted. The truth was that Veronica never felt more affectionate towards Alan than when they were forced to be apart. It was a glorious pain, missing him. Veronica sat and thought lovingly about her husband as the train left Sheffield and rushed down through the countryside towards London.

She had planned to go to Bruce's straight from the station to get changed before the meeting but, with the train delayed, she had no choice but to take a taxi from Paddington to South Kensington, having brushed her hair and reapplied some makeup in the train's loo.

The producer's office was a flat on the top floor of a stucco-fronted townhouse, a couple of roads south of the Natural History Museum. The buzzer had a handwritten sign that just read 'Felix'. She took a long breath to calm her nerves and buzzed. When the door clicked open, Veronica entered the hallway and made her way up the stairs to flat A. There was a baby's pram on the second-floor landing and a bicycle and wellies on the third. By the time she'd reached the top floor she could hear a piano playing and tried to settle her breathing. This was the place.

Felix de Foe was a self-proclaimed impresario. He had built a reputation as a Master of Ceremonies at one of the last Music Hall theatres still putting on five shows a week in the West End. He staged concerts all around England and sometimes even on the Continent. According to Veronica's agent, he was always looking for good singers. Veronica had been told that he was eccentric, and she was glad that she had been forewarned. As she pushed through the door with a polite 'hello?', she saw him hunched over a baby grand that took up most of the room. The curtains were still drawn, the room cluttered with boxes, sheet music and a variety of objects – some that could have been props and costumes for a show, others that could have been piles of dirty laundry.

Felix got to the end of the song's phrase and raised his head. He didn't sit up straight. He stepped off the piano stool and, retaining his C-shaped stance, stepped towards her and reached out his hand.

'I'm Veronica Craig,' she held out her hand to shake his. In one fluent move, Felix grasped her fingers, turned the hand over and kissed her wrist, holding his lips long enough that she was given time to inspect the top of his wispy-bald head and yellowing crease of his shirt collar.

'A great pleasure it is to meet you,' he said.

Veronica set down her suitcase and reached into her handbag for sheet music. 'I thought I'd do "Has Anyone Here Seen Kelly", if that works for you,' she said.

'All in good time, songbird.' Felix took the pages from her and slapped them on top of the piano which was already covered with other scores, a few burned down candles and a bowl with a dried crust of tomato soup. 'First, tea.'

He moved towards one of the bookcases and leaned his weight against it. It moved inwards, revealing a dark little kitchen and another person, slouched at the counter reading.

'Two teas, Reggie,' he said.

The man in the kitchen looked up from his magazine and nodded. Reggie was younger than Felix and taller. Although almost anyone would look taller than Felix. Handsome, with floppy red hair, flared jeans, a patterned shirt and a waistcoat with tassels, Reggie looked over to Veronica and winked.

Felix moved back to his piano leaving the door to the kitchen open, enabling Veronica to watch Reggie move around, removing tea bags from the caddy and flipping them into the air before catching them in the pot. Reggie arranged two cups on a tray and took a pair of teaspoons from the dresser drawer, tapping a little rhythm before balancing each on its saucer. He took a biscuit tin off the shelf and opened it carefully, as if something could spring out of it, looking at Veronica, in fake disgust after he'd snapped it closed. Veronica laughed.

'Cookies are arf,' he said in a juicy American accent.

'Well, go to the shop and get some more, you bloody idiot,' snapped Felix. 'What am I paying you for?'

Reggie sidled into the living room and held out his hand to Felix, who fished in a pocket for change. As he struggled to reach the coins, Felix's trousers moved up his legs and Veronica noticed that he was wearing spats. Eventually on retrieving three pennies, he placed them in Reggie's outreached palm.

'Now off you go, naughty boy,' he said. 'And you returning some time today would be ideal, if that's not too inconvenient.'

Once Reggie had left, the idea of tea was forgotten, and the cups and tray remained in the kitchen undisturbed. Felix wanted to discuss exactly what he was looking for.

'You're too old for an ingénue,' he began.

'I'm only 28,' Veronica protested.

'Oh, that's even older than I thought,' he continued. 'You funny?'

'Oh, well, yes, I've had experience with comedy roles. I played the wicked fairy in the panto last year and...'

'Let's hear the pipes,' he swivelled in place until his hands reached the keys. '"Oh, Oh Antonio" in E flat – will that do?' But he was already playing the intro. Without any time to protest, Veronica began.

In the dark, airless room, she gave it her all, singing out as if she was in a concert hall. Veronica's voice was warm and saucy, the song unfolded effortlessly, and she felt confident enough to act out the character's frustration and comic anger. '*Left me alone-io, all on my own-io...*" An image of Bobbi popped into her head and Veronica imagined that, if her friend could see her now, she'd surely comment on the aura that must be bursting from her and lighting up the dreary room. Veronica didn't notice Reggie return or see him standing, watching, leaning against the front door frame with a pack of rich tea biscuits tucked under his arm and a big smile on his face. As she finished, Felix performed a flourish on the piano, then spun around to her. Veronica was a little out of breath. Her hands, which had been raised for the final note, dropped to her side and she looked at him for a response.

Before Felix could give his feedback, Reggie blurted, "That was magic. What a gift you have. I'm so glad I got back in time to hear you. That was *magic*."

Felix was miffed. 'Young man, your tea making abilities are required, not your opinion."

Veronica smiled at Reggie, who slinked back to the kitchen unfazed.

'A gift can be a curse if you don't know how to use it,' said Felix. 'But I think I can help you. What are you doing tonight?' he said, hopping off the piano stool and moving to the other side of the room to lean again on one of the bookcases. This hidden door was a little harder to shift and he pressed against it for a moment before stepping back and taking a run-up. His shoulder made a thud and the bookcase moved back to reveal another room.

'Tonight?' said Veronica. 'I'm staying with a friend in Notting Hill Gate, but I suppose I could...'

'There's a spot for you at a cabaret I'm doing at Talk of the

Town. Two songs – maybe three. Got one poor gal down with the flu – or so she says.' Felix disappeared into the second room.

Veronica stood alone and waited. She could hear Reggie filling the kettle in the kitchen. She looked around at the peculiar museum of a living-room she found herself in. There wasn't a visible patch of wall space as every inch was filled, either with a bulging bookcase or a framed picture of a Music Hall performer. Some of the photographs could have been Felix, some were obviously famous names from the past, Marie Lloyd, Florrie Forde, Hetty King.

'Are you coming?' Felix called from the other room.

Veronica gingerly stepped into it. Also dark, it was filled with costumes piled haphazardly from floor to ceiling and smelled of mildew and old sweat. Felix was rummaging through the pile nearest to a sealed-up window.

'I'm storing them all in here temporarily,' he said without looking up. 'I had to move them out of the last theatre in a bit of a hurry and haven't had the chance to get them organised.'

Felix reached what he was looking for, a green and white bodice in the Music Hall style. 'This is it,' he said. He threw it over to Veronica and then dove once again into the pile, looking for the skirt. When he it found it at the bottom of the stack of clothes, it was stuck to the carpet and he peeled it off with care before shaking it free and spraying mildew spores across the room. 'Shoe size?'

'Maybe I can wear my own,' said Veronica lamely.

Felix looked down at the black-strapped heels she was wearing. 'Not an impossible idea. OK, try this on and we'll see how you look.'

Felix left Veronica in the stinky room and went back to his piano. He started playing another tune. Veronica held up the skirt and opened it to step in. She could see the clasp was broken and she'd have to sew on a couple of buttons that were hanging loose from the front panel. She pulled it up around her waist, over the top of the dress she was wearing, and looked up. Felix's eyes were just visible over the top of the piano, watching her as she changed.

'I'll take this,' she said, dropping the skirt, stepping out of it and taking hold of the bodice. 'I'll need to make a few alterations to the fastening if that's OK.'

'Suit yourself,' said Felix looking down to his keyboard again as he wasn't going to get the opportunity to watch her undress.

With the dress packed into her case, Veronica said her goodbyes. Reggie stuck his head around the kitchen doorway and beamed a smile at her.

'Take these three songs,' Felix said, handing over some sheet music. 'Get there for 6pm for a run through. I've written the address down for you. Reggie will meet you at the stage door.'

Reggie gave a little wave.

'Reggie?' asked Veronica.

'He's the piano. So, you know him already. He'll introduce you to everyone else.'

'Oh good.'

'If all goes well, I can sign you up for three shows a week, at least, and perhaps a tour in December. I doubt very much that my other singer is returning. I think she's pregnant. You're not pregnant, are you?'

'Oh, no, no I'm not.'

Felix started tickling the piano keys again and Veronica took this as a signal to leave. She gathered up her bags, the music and headed out. As she pulled the front door closed she could hear Felix telling off Reggie, 'You will turn my hair grey, you silly thing." Veronica skipped down the stairs to the ground level.

With a job in London she could move here. She hadn't been cast in *The Cherry Orchard* so didn't have much to keep her in Sheffield career-wise. She'd need to find somewhere to rent that was big enough for her, the girls and Audrey. Maybe Bruce would help with that? As for Alan, she was pretty sure he'd support the move. This was an opportunity for her to sing in London and potentially get a London agent, like Bruce had. Veronica stepped out onto the street and took a fresh look around. This could be her city.

V

By the time Veronica's third child, and Alan's fourth, was born, they had lived in London for three years. Veronica had worked with Felix de Foe for a few months, but it had been her casting in a TV crime serial that had given them the money and impetus to make London their permanent home. Alan commuted between London and Sheffield as required and even signed on with a London-based agent himself. They hadn't been able to persuade Audrey to join them as they had hoped. She had fallen in love with one of her boyfriends and was planning on getting married. Instead they hired a Spanish student, Marisol, to look after the girls, and ferry them to and from nursery school. They had rented a large flat in Lancaster Gate and it even came with a hard-working cleaning lady, Mrs Terzi, who was uncomplaining about the kids' mess or the occasional house guest crashed out on one of the sofas. Having a big flat in central London and lots of friends in Sheffield did make for a steady stream of visitors.

When Veronica realised she was pregnant with her third child, the timing was hardly perfect. Her contract with the crime series was up for renewal and she fretted about how long she could keep the pregnancy secret in order to secure the work for a few more months at least. Her agent, Peter Dennis, wasn't very encouraging.

'They took a risk with you as an unknown,' Peter said when they met over tea in a local caff. 'I think the best you can expect is to disappear out of the next series and hopefully get to return once the baby's born and you're back in shape.'

Veronica was disappointed, but she trusted his judgement. Signing up with Peter Dennis had been the best move she'd ever made, especially when he secured her an audition for *Operation 999*. Veronica had been introduced to him after a gig with Felix de Foe and things had moved pretty quickly from first meeting to first audition to first job. Peter was entertaining, a handsome guy, with a seemingly inexhaustible list of contacts in the business.

From the first job, Peter had been slow in paying although Veronica hadn't complained. From what she heard from Bruce, it wasn't standard for an agent to hold onto an artist's money for a period of time like Peter did. However, Veronica was being paid, albeit after a bit of a wait, so she decided against bringing it up. With the pregnancy and her having to leave *Operation 999*, it was pretty low on the list of priorities to discuss.

Peter called the waitress over and asked for another cup of tea.

'I think you should do radio.' He filled up his cup with one spoonful of sugar after another. 'The BBC studio is pretty close to where you live, and you can be whatever size you want on radio.'

'Singing?' she asked

'Maybe, but also I was thinking about a radio play or two.'

'Yes, I could do that.'

Peter looked at his watch, lifted the still-steaming cup to his lips and drained it. 'I've got to run. I'll speak to *999* and break the news and then let's look at what radio work's available.'

'Thanks so much, Pete,' Veronica said. 'I'm really sorry about this. It wasn't exactly how I planned things.'

Peter stood, slipped his coat on and blew her a kiss. 'Onwards and upwards,' he said, exiting.

Veronica watched him walk down the street towards the tube. She felt a little better knowing that she could still work. Alan's own contract was coming to an end in Sheffield, so money would be tight even before the next baby came.

Veronica looked down at the two empty cups. The bill had been left on the table. That was pretty typical of Peter. She picked it up and walked to the counter to pay.

As Veronica and the girls were now in London and Alan was there at least once a week, it was hard to find excuses to avoid Bunny. She would pop around when she knew Alan was in town for the day, which cut into the time Veronica had alone with her husband. Veronica had given up keeping quiet about it.

'It's probably better if you come for Sunday lunch and then leave straight afterwards,' Veronica told Bunny on the phone.

'It would be more convenient for me to come this evening actually,' she replied. 'I promised a friend that I'd go and see them on Sunday, and they put their children to bed early.'

'It's not going to work for us this evening,' said Veronica. 'Maybe we should just give it a miss this week.'

'If you refuse to budge, I'll tell them I can't see them,' huffed Bunny. 'They won't be pleased but that's just too bad. You see, they are strict about bedtimes.'

'We're strict about bedtimes.' Veronica felt insulted immediately. Every conversation she had with Bunny followed along these lines, Veronica feeling judged. The attack was subtle, but it was always there, whether for her parenting, her support of her husband or her own ambitions.

'Your house is chaos, dear,' Bunny continued. 'My friend is someone who puts her family first.'

'How can you say I don't put my family first?' Veronica was angrier that she had been for a long time.

'No need to take offence. It's different for my friend. She gave up work when she had children. She could have been a marvellous pianist but gave it all up.'

'I can't listen to any more of this,' said Veronica. 'Come over or don't come over, I don't care.'

She hung up. That was the first time she'd hung up on Bunny and she knew that she'd have to explain it to Alan, who was expected to arrive that afternoon. It was such a cliché to argue with your mother-in-law, and she'd bent over backwards to make Bunny feel comfortable and welcome but she just couldn't do it any longer. In the hope of calming herself, Veronica grabbed her handbag, ran a comb through her hair and left the flat.

It was a bright spring day and she walked down the Bayswater Road towards Queensway with the sun on her face. She brushed angry tears out of her eyes as she strode along. She hated how Alan held Bunny up as the epitome of the perfect mother when all she did was criticise Veronica and fawn over Alan. 'With everything I have on my shoulders I should get more respect,' Veronica told herself. She got minimal help with the girls, and she was trying to build her own career too. She was someone to be admired, not admonished.

Veronica took a right turn onto Queensway and passed the ice rink. Two kids were sitting on the pavement outside.

'Got any money, missus?' one said.

She shook her head and walked on.

Veronica knew that she had everything she needed to make it as a serious actress. But why did she have to do it with so much responsibility, the flat to manage, the girls to look after, entertaining Alan's dreadful mother and now another baby on the way too? She felt the imaginary weight bearing down on her actual shoulders. If she could only have stayed at *Operation 999* for another year. That would have cemented her reputation as a TV actress. She could have made some money and perhaps saved up enough to buy a flat. Would Marisol stay once she found out that another baby was on the way and she'd have to look after three kids?

Veronica entered Whiteleys as if she had always meant it as her destination. The department store was way past its prime and large bright banners announcing a cut-price sale had been in place for months. The overly-enthusiastic ads, now dusty, hung without promise over the sad, empty store. Shop assistants leant on their counters, bored, waiting for custom. The miserable strip-lights and out-of-date fashions somehow quieted Veronica. Seeing rows of grotty mannequins like sad old relics in the world's worst museum, she felt the pressure of her judgemental mother-in-law dissipate. Veronica walked up to a crate of silk scarves, picked one up and ran it through her hands a couple of times.

There was nothing she could do now. No clever footwork that would get her to where she wanted to be. She was trapped, and she'd just have to deal with it. Her agent, Peter, had seemed pretty confident about radio work and she'd just have to be more adamant with him about paying her on time. She shouldn't have to ask him for cash like she was a kid asking for pocket money. Veronica moved towards the perfume counter and reached forward to spritz herself with a potion called 'Midnight in Paris'. She'd try and tell Alan exactly what she felt. That his mother was making her life miserable. That he should deal with her himself and see her on his own. The woman didn't seem to care one bit for her granddaughters or her daughter-in-law. And what had Bunny achieved anyway? What had Bunny done that was so remarkable that it put her up on a pedestal, looking down on everyone else?

It was close to four o'clock and, calmed by her time in the second-rate store, Veronica decided to trek home. As she reached the exit, a hand was placed on her shoulder.

'Madam, can you come with me?' It was one of the Whiteley's security guards.

'Excuse me?' Veronica said. 'I'm just leaving.'

'I don't think you are, madam. Not without paying for that scarf.'

One of the scarves was still wrapped around her neck, a guilty looking snake of synthetic silk that the security guard was pointing to. She removed it laughing.

'Oh, that was a mistake, I'm not buying that.'

'I need you to come with me to the back office, madam.'

The back office was a colourless room with a desk too large and too many chairs to make an efficient interrogation space. A pin-board had a list of rules for staff, an emergency telephone number and a saucy postcard stuck on it. Veronica was ushered into a plastic chair.

'There's been a mistake,' she said again. 'I wasn't trying to steal the scarf.'

'Our store detective has been following you for forty-five minutes and you didn't at any point make an attempt to pay before leaving.'

'I forgot I was wearing it,' Veronica replied in a voice that was already cracking.

'They often say that.' This statement came from a short man in a suit who was standing in the doorway with his hands in his pockets. He looked like a miniature gangster and smirked like he was enjoying himself.

Before the interrogation could go further, the store detective took Veronica's handbag and poked around inside, plucking out random objects and laying them on the table. Although everything belonged to Veronica, the purse, the makeup compact, the keys, the packet of tissues, he lined them up purposefully and nodded with each item as if his accusations were being confirmed. Veronica started to cry. She was angry at herself for letting her emotions show so obviously, so pathetically, but it all seemed so unfair. She couldn't answer any questions as she spluttered into her hankie, she could barely breathe. Wave after wave of emotion poured over her and she gasped for air, looking up at the security guard in despair.

'Is there anyone I can call?' said the store's security guard who seemed embarrassed by the outpouring from his prisoner.

'I'd call the police,' said the gangster store detective. 'Don't be taken in by the waterworks.'

'Shut up, Mikey,' the security guard reached over to the phone and pushed it in front of Veronica. A grey phone in a grey office. He picked up the receiver, sticky from greasy fingers, and handed it to her.

Not knowing if Alan would have arrived in the flat at that point, or if it would be Marisol who would answer, she dialled. When Alan's voice came over the line she was relieved but couldn't get a word out and was forced to hand the phone back to the security guard.

A quick explanation over the phone brought Alan down to the store to pick up his hysterical wife and sort it all out.

The security guard, now firmly in the role of 'good cop', poured Veronica a coffee from the crude-oil black liquid that had been lingering at the bottom of a percolator. Veronica sipped it and felt a bit better. She knew Alan was on his way. Like he'd done with the critic who accused her of being badly cast in the role of wicked fairy, he'd take these guys to task. He'd stick up for her and that little Edward G. Robinson in his nasty suit would be forced to apologise.

But when Alan came he was full of apologies himself. He shook the gangster's hand and thanked the security guard for calling him. He moved towards Veronica like she was a naughty child in the headmaster's office and shook his head. He watched as she packed her belongings back into her handbag; then, after a shared glance and smile with the gangster store detective, he led her out of the room and out of the store.

They were silent as they waited for the bus to take them down Bayswater Road and back home.

'Why didn't you stand up for me?' she asked eventually.

'Let's just put this all behind us.' Alan said, hailing a bus and stepping back so that she could get on first.

'I wasn't in the wrong and you took their side.' Veronica's voice was trembling again.

'You're pregnant,' he said without much warmth. 'You're not thinking straight.'

'That little bastard acted like I was a master criminal.'

'Let's not continue this conversation,' said Alan without looking at his wife. 'You don't mean what you're saying.'

'Fuck you,' Veronica said quietly. And she meant it.

The radio jobs didn't come as Veronica had hoped and even the auditions dried up. However, they still had some money in the bank from *Operation 999* and Alan's stint at The Lyceum, so it wasn't time to panic yet. Egged on by a drunken late-night conversation with friends, Alan and Veronica decided to "go private" for the birth of their next child. It felt like a treat. Veronica was checked in as Mrs Tomlinson, had a private room and, when the contractions started, an epidural.

It wasn't just the birth that was painless. Veronica was overjoyed with her healthy son, received visits from her friends and stayed in a room full of flowers. Big Veronica was in town to help Marisol with the two little ones and she brought them to the hospital with Alan each day for the four days that Veronica stayed there being waited on and fussed over by nurses.

Despite some initial jealousy, Veronica's daughters did enjoy their brother and rushed in each day from school to check on him. Alan, now free from his contract in Sheffield, was in London looking for work so, for the first time ever, the family spent an extended period of time together. Even Bunny, overjoyed at having another male to add to the Tomlinson family tree, was less annoying and occasionally even praised Veronica for how well the baby slept and ate and moved his chubby little hands, 'like a conductor'.

After one great Easter Sunday involving treasure hunts around the flat, overseen by Bunny, a huge paella cooked by Marisol and songs around the piano courtesy of their guest, Reggie, who was now Veronica's official accompanist and one of the regulars at the flat, Alan suggested going for a walk as a group to Hyde Park.

'I was thinking we could pop around and drop a note in for Peter Dennis,' he said, and Veronica could see that he was already holding one of his trademark theatrical postcards and a fountain pen.

'Really?' she said.

'The thing is,' he was speaking under his breath now, as Marisol and Bunny bustled the kids into their coats and pram, 'he hasn't paid you for months and we're almost tapped out.'

'He still owes me from 999.'

'Yeah, that's what I'm hoping. I know you've tried to call him, but with him not picking up the phone, I thought on Easter Sunday he might be at home, or at least we'd know he'd got the note and couldn't ignore it.'

Kensington Gardens was lively with families and they stopped by the Peter Pan statue to count up the little animals they could see in bronze. The girls chased around the statue, dragging Reggie.

'Look, there's a snail,' said Natalie.

'Yuck,' said Reggie. 'I hate snails. Who can find me a mouse?'

As the group moved to check out the fish in the Italian Gardens, Alan decided it was time for their mission to see Peter Dennis.

'We'll meet you at home,' he said, 'We've just got to drop in on a friend.'

'What's all this about?' Bunny asked.

Veronica just shook her head. 'Don't worry, it's nothing. How about we take a photo before we head off?'

Reggie offered to do the honours and the family group lined up, Veronica fixing her hair and dabbing on lipstick before picking the baby from his pram and holding him up in the sunlight.

'Say fleas,' said Reggie and the girls laughed.

'It's cheese,' corrected Natalie.

'Not if you live with Felix de Foe, it's not.'

Veronica tucked her arm in her husband's as they strode off, leaving the children with their grandmother, their nanny and one of their surrogate 'aunties', Reggie, who was lining them up for a second photograph.

'There's so little work,' Alan said as they walked along the line of paintings hanging on the railings by the park. 'There's an assistant director position going in Australia, but I don't see that as something I should be doing right now.'

They looked at the gaudy pictures as they walked along. Most of the artists, who sat beside their work on camp chairs with thermos flasks in their laps, were trying to shift unconvincing replicas of great masters, with thick goops of paint slapped on canvas to represent Van Gogh, or miniature Turner landscapes copied without much precision from an image on top of a box of fancy biscuits. Some artists had worked in metal to build skinny statuettes of clowns riding bicycles or sea lions balancing balls on their snouts.

Veronica and Alan stopped at one painting, a brightly coloured scene of two little girls standing in a field of sunflowers. 'I like this,' Veronica said. 'It reminds me of the girls.'

'Yes, I see what you mean.' He stood inspecting the picture as if he was at an important gallery. He rested his hand in his chin and leaned forward. 'It's just like Natalie and Alice.'

The artist, who had been lounging in the camper van that was parked in front of his spot, noticed a potential customer and leapt out to introduce himself.

'This is a popular piece,' he said, standing beside it proudly. 'I'd be sad to see it go. It's five pounds if you want to take it right now.'

'Not that sad then?' said Alan, reaching into his back jeans pocket for his wallet.

'Can we afford it?' said Veronica.

'If we live on baked beans on toast for a month.'

So, with the large painting, wrapped in paper, carried under Alan's arm, they turned onto Porchester Terrace where Peter Dennis lived. His flat was in a modern block, squeezed into the space left by a Blitz bomb, the one brown building in a row of white houses. They buzzed and waited.

After a few repeated buzzes and a long enough wait to ascertain that Peter Dennis wasn't answering, they pressed the porter's button.

'What?' The answer was immediate.

'Umm, we're looking for Peter Dennis,' Alan said.

'Aren't we all?' came the distorted voice through the speaker.

'Can we leave a note for him, perhaps?'

'Look, he's scarpered, mate. That's all I can tell you. There's been one person after another coming around here looking for money. He owed me too. He did a flit about three weeks ago and he owes me for rent dating right back to I wouldn't like to say.'

'He's gone?' Veronica was staggered.

'He ain't here and you're welcome to check his flat, like some of the others who came 'round and wouldn't take no for no answer. But I'm telling you all that he left me with was an old mattress, half a fondue set and a pile of dirty magazines.'

'I'm sorry,' said Veronica.

A click came from the buzzer signalling that the porter had

hung up.

Veronica wasn't angry; that would come later. She was just worried about their next move. Alan struggled with the slightly too large painting and ended up resting it on his head as he walked beside his wife, his arms stretched out in an awkward Y.

'Well, Australia might be nice. Do you know anything about the theatre?' Veronica said. 'Do you get to put on your own shows or just assist? Because, if you could do your own thing, it might be worth considering.'

'I'll send them a letter tomorrow,' he replied.

When they returned home, Reggie was playing the piano and Bruce had arrived and was singing a song for the girls. Baby Alexander was asleep in a carrycot on top of the piano as Reggie played.

'Where's Marisol?' Veronica looked into the cot at the baby who was sleeping peacefully despite the vibrations and noise.

'She went on a date,' said Natalie. 'And Granny is fixing us some leftovers.'

Alan ripped the paper off the picture and presented it to the group. The children cheered.

'Can you tell it's you?' He leaned it on the mantlepiece and stood back. 'Suits this spot, I think.'

'*Two little maids from school are we,*' Bruce started singing and Reggie picked up the tune.

Veronica stood watching her family. Alan was leaning against the wall gazing at the painting seemingly in another world in front of a field of sunflowers, Natalie was clapping along to the song and Alice was sitting with a big smile and wide eyes, watching her sister rocking to and fro as the beat sped up. So, maybe they'd move to Australia? Maybe some job would come in and they'd stay in London? They both needed to work to keep this circus going. This happy, creative, funny old circus that was her family.

VI

By Alexander's 10th birthday, all memories of Mrs Terzi's

occupation had been well and truly forgotten. The kids barely remembered Australia, and Veronica lived in the Lancaster Gate flat carefree, with the occasional lodger and every few months a visit from Alan, who had extended his contract multiple times as he rose to Artistic Director at the South Australian theatre company. It was rare that anyone even reminded her of that chaotic time when she'd returned to London with the kids and found her flat squatted.

Veronica had been working pretty steadily for a few years, taking parts in a variety of West End musicals, some that opened and closed in a matter of months and others that ran and ran. The family's financial security rose and fell in perfect harmony with the box office success of these shows. Sometimes she'd take the kids on an extravagant holiday, other times she'd coach them on what to say if bailiffs arrived when she was at work.

Veronica had made friends with the two women who lived directly below. Eileen and Dawn had recently moved in and came up often to borrow utensils for cooking or tools to repair their flat, which seemed like it hadn't been decorated in decades. When either of them ventured upstairs, Veronica always invited them to stay for a cup of coffee. Although she had never asked them to one of her Sunday lunch parties, which now had a reputation amongst the London theatre crowd, she did spend quite a bit of time with them, listening to their stories which fascinated, amused and horrified her. Together Eileen and Dawn managed a dungeon in Paddington providing a much-in-demand service for grown men who appreciated being treated like disobedient heretics.

Eileen was in her late 50s, with close-cropped curly hair and glasses that took up a large part of her face. She dressed in unflattering wash n' wear trouser-suits and wore an anorak year-round. Her flatmate, colleague and true love, was the glamorous one of the pair. With a Farrah Fawcett flick on her auburn hair, fitted jeans and bright button earrings, 47-year old Dawn could easily be mistaken for being many years younger. It was Dawn who administered the punishment at work. Eileen, described by

Dawn as 'one of the best maids in the business', had the job of taking bookings and moving punters from entrance to waiting room to torture chamber to shower to exit without coming into contact with any other paying guest. Both were adamant that they never had sex with their clients and never would.

'Since we've put the rack in, we've been run off our feet,' said Dawn one day when they were both upstairs with Veronica showing off the little dog they'd just picked up from Battersea Dogs' Home.

'We had it built special and it's a beauty,' confirmed Eileen. 'Not a bit of bother with it.'

'So I have a question for you,' said Veronica, taking the pup into her lap. 'How do the men explain away the marks you leave on them?'

'That's their bloody problem,' said Dawn. 'Although most of what I do is threaten rather than actually hit them. I create an air of impending peril,' she said grandly. 'And that works for me too. Since I had that shoulder thing, I've been trying to keep the whipping to a minimum.'

'You're an actress,' said Veronica.

'Yes, but she plays the same part every day,' said Eileen.

'And the audience has to have a shower before they go home.' Her girlfriend laughed loudly enough that it startled the dog into barking.

Before they could settle the dog, they heard the front door slam as the three children arrived home from school, the teenage girls yelling a hello before disappearing into their own rooms, Alex running into the kitchen asking about when they were having tea. He stopped in his tracks at the sight of the dog.

'Is that puppy for us?'

''fraid not, kiddiwink,' said Eileen. 'But you can come downstairs and see him whenever you like.'

'Can I take him for a walk?' Alexander was on his knees in front of the dog on his mother's lap.

'Sure you can,' said Dawn. 'Look, why don't you take him now and show him to your sisters. His name is Fang.'

Alex trotted off with the dog, calling out to his sisters as he went, 'you will not believe what I have here...'

'Alan's back this weekend,' said Veronica. 'It's been four months and the kids are very excited. Alex wants to go and pick him up at the airport. I've been trying to explain that it's a very early flight. I'm hoping that Alan's going to finish up in Australia after this contract comes to an end. It'd be good to have him here for a while and no more of those terrible long flights.'

'You have one of those marriages where you don't need to be under each other's feet,' said Dawn. 'You don't have to escape each other like some of our punters.'

'Well, I bloody hope not,' said Veronica.

'Once you understand what a guy wants it's pretty easy to please them, I've found,' Dawn continued. 'And what they want is always straightforward. And when you're done with that, they can't leave quick enough.'

'Best to stay out of each other's way,' said Eileen, who was picking up the mugs and teapot and taking them to the sink for a rinse. 'Men and women were not designed to live in each other's pockets.'

'Eileen was married once,' said Dawn.

'It was many moons ago.' She tipped the cups upside down to drain on the side. 'I consider it a low point.'

'And you, Dawn, have you ever been married?' asked Veronica.

Dawn stood and walked over to Eileen, swinging her arm around her waist. 'She's the only husband I need.'

'You're a floozy,' said Eileen smiling. 'Go fetch the mutt and let's go home.'

Everyone was in a heightened state when Alan arrived very early on Sunday morning. Veronica had been yelling at the kids all Saturday to help her clean the flat and prepare for a wonderful Sunday lunch, just with the family this time. They all got up early and there was tension in the air as they sat around the table waiting for him to arrive.

'Now, don't all leap on him at once,' she said, trying to lighten the mood. 'He'll be tired. We don't want to scare him away.'

Alan entered and, ignoring his mother's warning, Alexander ran to hug him. Alan was carrying a small rucksack which surprised Veronica as they'd spoken about him bringing over more and more of his things with each trip to save the cost of shipping everything at the end of his contract.

He unzipped the bag and removed presents for the kids. Although the gifts were not anything that the teenage girls or 10-year-old boy would want, a remote-controlled fire-truck for Alexander and boxes of embroidered handkerchiefs for the girls, the kids made a good show of being grateful and Alex tore around the flat looking for an electric device he could rob of its batteries.

Alice, who had always been the quiet one was the most changed from Alan's previous visit. She said she was going to try out for a part in the school play and questioned her father about whether he'd help her prepare her audition.

'Sure, what's the play?' he asked.

'*The Importance of Being Earnest.*'

'Of course, it is,' he said.

Veronica was making coffee and watching them all. It was good to see Alan take an interest in Alice, for them to have a common ground.

'And how is "The Voice"?' Alan asked turning in his chair to look at Veronica.

'No one's called me that in years,' she smiled. 'But thanks for remembering.'

'The show's going OK?'

'We start rehearsals on Thursday. I've got a costume fitting next week too so I'm slimming… again.'

'You look beautiful.' he said, and she smiled wider still.

After a snooze, he joined them for lunch and then suggested that the kids take a walk.

'Can't you come with us, Dad?' Alexander said urgently. 'We

could take the remote-controlled car.'

Natalie stepped in. 'Leave Dad alone. We'll go, and we can take the car – it would be interesting to see what range it has.'

With the kids out of the way, Veronica was a little giddy. It felt like old times when they had to sneak around to see each other and capture moments alone when they could.

'Another glass of wine?' she said. 'Or coffee perhaps? Or maybe we should just go to bed for a while, until the kids get back?'

'Coffee would be great,' he said.

He was silent for a bit and watched her move around the kitchen.

'They've offered me another extension on the contract,' he said eventually.

Veronica was disappointed. 'You're not going to take it though, are you?'

'I think it makes sense. What do I have to come back for?'

'Well, me and the kids.' She was angry.

'I mean work-wise,' he said. 'This is a rock-solid salary and what's the likelihood of me getting that in London at the moment?'

'But the kids are almost grown up and you're missing so much.'

'I see them when I can. They understand that.'

'Do they?'

'Like you say, they're almost grown up. They're not babies anymore. And I've got to go where the work is. I'm trying to create something really special in Adelaide. A theatre that's way ahead of anything else available in the state, maybe the country.'

'I'm just disappointed, that's all.' Veronica remembered Bunny's warning not to stand in his way. Veronica put the coffee cup down in front of him. She couldn't think of anything to say that wouldn't turn this conversation into an argument, which she didn't want on his first day back.

'Actually, I don't think I'll have coffee. Just going to have a lie down. Jet-lag's kicking in.'

'We can talk about this later, though, right?'

'Of course. Nothing's set in stone.'

With the flat to herself, Veronica put on a record and stretched out on the sofa. She was listening to the record that Alan had bought her so long ago, a little scratched now and she had to get up now and again to nudge the needle onwards. The record didn't stir up the same tender feelings that it used to anymore. 'Leaving on a Jet Plane' seemed less about returning to wear a wedding ring and more about being let down and disappearing. Maybe this was the status quo. She was expected to be there as needed when Alan returned but they'd never live together as a regular couple. She didn't wait until the record reached its end, instead put it back in its sleeve and flipped through her collection for something less evocative.

After a day of catching up on his sleep, Alan went to visit his son, John, who had left his mother's home and was living in a bedsit in West Hampstead. It had been years since John had been around to the Lancaster Gate flat and he hadn't seen his brother and sisters in such a long time. They rarely asked about him anymore.

Veronica went to the theatre to meet the costume designer, as planned, and try on the dress that had been made for her. She didn't like it but wrestled between getting what she wanted and being declared difficult. She asked if she could take it home with her and perhaps take it in a little around the shoulders for a better fit. The costume designer shrugged and told her to do as she pleased. There were 30 costumes to be made for this production and work was backing up already. She didn't care.

Veronica took the bus home. Her first pay check wouldn't come in for a few weeks and they were 'battening down the hatches' until then. She entered the flat as Eileen was leaving with her dog, Fang.

'How's he doing?' she asked, leaning over to pet the pup.

'Oh, he's a right one,' said Eileen proudly. 'Has us wrapped around his little paw. Dawn even wants to take him to work as he hates to be left on his own.'

Veronica laughed. 'Well, you can always leave him with me. Once the show's started I'll be here most days.'

She entered her flat and put her costume in its bag on the piano stool. As she moved towards the kitchen, she noticed an envelope propped up on the mantlepiece leaning against the painting of the two girls in the sunflower field. It was addressed to her in Alan's handwriting. She opened it immediately and saw that it was a postcard of Lawrence Oliver and Vivien Leigh from *Fire Over England*. She smiled. She imagined she was getting a love letter. This was usually his style. But the letter was different from any of the others he'd sent her.

My darling, you will always have a place in my heart, but I've decided to stay in Australia. I've become close to a woman in the company and although I never wanted this to happen, I can't deny that things have changed between us. Life moves in curious ways, 'a tale told by an idiot', but I know that you and the children will be fine. I won't have time to say goodbye to the children. Please give them a kiss from me and let them know that I'll come and see them whenever I'm in London. Good luck with your first night. I'm sorry I'm not going to see it. It sounds like a wonderful show.

That was it. Blue-inked words squeezed onto the back of a postcard. Veronica sat on the floor in front of the fireplace and tried to breathe. What was she going to do? How was she going to keep everything going? She didn't want to be divorced. She'd kept up this façade of a relationship with Alan for years, but she couldn't accept that it was something that meant so little to him.

When Natalie came in from school, Veronica was still sitting on the floor, in front of the fireplace. She was in a daze.

'Mum?' her daughter stood over her. 'Are you not feeling well?'

'Dad and I are getting a divorce.'

Natalie's lips tightened into a scowl. 'Fuck him,' she said.

'Natalie, please.'

'I mean it, Mum. Who the fuck is he anyway? Don't tell me he wants to fight you over custody?'

Veronica looked up and found herself smiling. 'Well, no, he didn't mention that.'

'Yeah, what a surprise?' her daughter said sarcastically, helping her mother to stand.

'Alexander will be upset.'

Natalie huffed. 'Yes, but he'll get used to it. He won't be missing much.'

'And Alice will be disappointed. They were finally getting to know each other.'

'She only wants him to help her become an actress. She can barely stand the guy.'

'What?' Veronica was genuinely surprised.

'Mum. Did you really think we were taken in by the happy family scene you and Dad have been acting out for us? We only usually see him once a year. He's like bloody Father Christmas – except less reliable.'

'Oh please,' Veronica was chuckling despite herself.

'And Alex is over Father Christmas now. He's too old for all that. Who needs another stupid fire truck? He'd rather have a BBC Micro.'

'I could get him one of those once the show starts.'

'And I could really do with new pair of shoes. You know, if you're buying consolation presents.'

'I'm alright, Jack, pull the ladder up.'

'And Alice wants a perm. You know a proper perm, done in a hairdressers.'

'What's all this going to cost me?'

'Send the bill to Dad,' said Natalie. 'Tell him we are devastated and need stuff to comfort us.'

'Devastated?'

'Oh, completely devastated.' Natalie put her hand to her forehead in a silent film dramatic gesture. 'You two are not the only ones who can act out their emotions.'

'The cops are becoming a bore.' Dawn was sitting, sipping tea in Veronica's kitchen, watching Eileen work the sewing machine on the kitchen table. Eileen struggled to push thick leatherette material under the needle. 'They all expect a five-finger discount.'

'What?' Veronica asked.

'They don't want to pay,' said Eileen without looking up.

'The dungeon is so convenient that we get a lot of drop-ins. Eileen's thinking of putting up another wall to split one of the waiting rooms in half so that we can have more of 'em lined up, you know? We certainly don't want any of our regulars seeing a cop in there waiting for his turn.'

Eileen took her foot off the pedal and held up the garment as Alice entered.

'What is that?' Alice said reaching out for the black leather top.

'It's meant to be a buzztiere.' Eileen handed it over.

'You pronounce it bustier,' said the girl.

'Oh, do you now?' Eileen laughed.

'Maybe I should wear something like this to my audition?' Alice held it across her body.

'I don't think so,' said Veronica. 'It's a bit sexy. His eyes would pop out of his head.'

Alice was looking to get hours towards her equity card and Felix de Foe had said that he might be able to find her something, but he'd insisted she come to his place so he could hear her sing and take a look at her. Eileen and Dawn were encouraging about the audition but offered advice about what to do if Felix tried anything.

'If you have the chance to keep the door open then, for fuck's sake, keep the door open.'

'She can handle herself,' said Veronica. 'But, they're right, stay one step ahead of him.'

'I thought he was gay.'

'He's a little rosy both ways, I've heard,' her mother warned.

When Alice went to her room to try on a few outfits, Eileen returned to her sewing, but Dawn wouldn't let the topic drop.

'Are you sure this is a good idea?' she said. 'You told us he was a dirty old man. Perhaps you should go with her.'

'It's the nature of the game, I'm afraid, and I am certainly not playing the role of stage mum. I might be going back to Felix myself begging for work if this show closes. Or I get replaced. It's not looking like this production will run for long and my agent has gone quiet on me. I could be joining the vast unemployed again.'

Once Alan agreed to pay for a boarding school for Alex, arrangements had to be made. Bunny, who for years had bragged that she could get any kid into any school because of her connections, did help secure an interview for Alexander at his father's old school in Kent. Veronica wasn't completely convinced that boarding school was a good idea. Alex had been positive when it had been suggested but he was a difficult kid to read. When she'd first told him about the divorce, he'd cried; but there was something about how quickly he'd recovered and how he never mentioned it again that made her think he was shedding tears because it was expected of him. She had asked him so many times if he was sure about going away to school, trying to ascertain if this was just another example of him hiding his true feelings. She was still none the wiser.

Boarding school had been Bruce's idea, suggesting it as a way of ensuring Alexander had enough straight male influence.

'The boy is surrounded by queens and dykes,' Bruce had said, and Veronica had felt defensive.

'That's not strictly true,' she'd objected.

'Get him to some old manor house, having cold showers and playing rugby.'

'You make it sound terrible.'

'It'll butch him up, that's for sure,' said Bruce.

Looking at the packing list together when it first arrived, they were tickled by the things it included, which seemed completely ludicrous when compared to anything either them had needed when they were at school in Sheffield.

'Mouth-guard, cricket box, penknife and study hall slippers,' Bruce read.

'No PJs?' Veronica asked.

'Pyjamas, two, and one flannel dressing gown. My point has been well and truly proven,' said Bruce smugly. 'We will make a man of him yet.'

She'd bought the lot from the school shop over the phone and it was due to arrive a few weeks before Alexander set off. He had surprised both her and his grandmother by insisting that neither of them took him to the station to meet the train. He said that he had asked John to be there to wait with him. It had taken Veronica a few seconds to realise that Alex was talking about his half-brother. She hadn't imagined that they had stayed in touch. When she mentioned it to Bruce he was even more delighted. It seemed his plan to get Alexander on a 'straight' path and away from his mummy's influence was taking shape already.

Bruce had opinions on each of Veronica's three children and he felt his role of honorary 'auntie' gave him the right and maybe even the duty to share his views. One night, when Veronica invited both Bruce and Alice to a midnight matinee, they went afterwards for a drink at a basement club popular with actors, and she could tell that they'd had words. Alice was sulking and, once through the door of The Green Room, the girl left them to get drinks and found herself a seat.

'What's up with her?' Veronica asked, as she watched her daughter slump into a sofa by the pool table.

'She wants to volunteer at the Terrence Higgins Trust,' said Bruce.

'OK?'

'I told her it was a terrible idea,' Bruce waved at the barman and held up three fingers. 'People will think she's a fag hag. She can't have that at the start of her career. She doesn't want anyone thinking she's too political.'

'She wants to help.'

'She's due to go off on that cruise ship in a month so what's the point anyway?'

The barman was taking his time pouring wine and the place was lively. Most of the actors who had been to the midnight matinee, a fundraiser for the Gay Men's Health Crisis, were now arriving at The Green Room and the place was getting full. Despite their being offstage and out of costume, it was easy to work out which actor was from which show. Handsome men with shiny quiffs stood together tapping their feet, itching to dance, a wistful guy with hair down his back was playing pool with a few disciples and members of a gospel choir were straddling chairs around a table telling stories that brought forth whoops of laughter and enthused clapping.

'I didn't want to say anything, but I think I saw one of the people you work with when we were leaving the stage door,' said Veronica.

Bruce looked concerned. 'Who?'

'One of the other teachers. Small, pretty, fat girl.'

He was relieved. 'Oh, that's Kay. Don't worry, she's not going to be a problem.'

Bruce's job as a drama teacher had been keeping the bills paid after acting work had dried up for him a couple of years earlier. It seemed unrealistic to Veronica that anyone could believe Bruce was straight and she didn't really understand why he had to keep up the charade in order to work there. But Bruce didn't want to risk being exposed. It was easier if he kept his private life private, he had said. It was a private school after all.

'Did she see us?' He reached over to pay the barman.

'Yes, you and Alice, just as I was coming out of the theatre.'

'Maybe she thinks we're a couple on a date.'

'What me and you?' Veronica slipped her arm through his, swishing the wine in the glasses he had picked up.

'Or me and Alice? You're a bit old for me.'

'Thanks for kicking a girl when she's down.' Veronica

relieved him of a glass and picked up the third which was on the bar for Alice.

'Only kidding, Vee,' he grinned. 'Now go and get Alice to smile, will you? I'm going to go and have a chat with Jesus over there. I've met him before. I think he and I even had a little thing when he first came to London.'

'I don't even know what to say to that,' she smiled. 'God's speed?'

The show Veronica was in closed within the month. She was back looking for the next gig and in the strange position of being at home listening to Alice rehearsing with Reggie as she prepared to join the chorus of a cruise ship on an eight-week tour. Alice would be flying into Miami to pick up the boat and entertaining hundreds of paying passengers on their trip around the Caribbean. She'd celebrate her seventeenth birthday on board. Alice had promised Veronica that she wouldn't go swimming in deep water, that she wouldn't take that risk, not after what they'd been through in Australia when she was a child. Felix de Foe had told them not to get too excited, that it wasn't exactly an all-singing all-dancing cruise, which was to be expected as this was Alice's first professional outing and, according to Felix, Alice had a rather weak voice and wasn't a great dancer.

With Alexander away at school until the holidays and Natalie at uni in Manchester, the house felt very different. Even Eileen and Dawn had been away for a few weeks, taking a holiday in Mallorca following a raid at the dungeon that freaked out a few of their regulars and got them both a date in court. Veronica was looking after their dog and spending more time in Hyde Park to avoid being in the flat waiting for the phone to ring. She was looking forward to the following weekend as Natalie was expected back for a couple of days and Veronica was planning a big Sunday lunch to welcome her home.

'She's bringing her new boyfriend,' she told Reggie when he was taking a break from the 'songs from the shows' medley he was working on with Alice.

'Fiancé,' said Alice, on the floor in the kitchen, stretching into splits as part of her exercises.

'What?'

'Oh, sorry, I've let the cat out the bag.' The girl laid her head down on her knees and stayed there, perhaps to avoid her mother's shocked expression. She groaned as she pulled her chin low and pointed her toes.

'She's engaged? She can't get married. This is ridiculous, I haven't even met the guy,' Veronica was standing over Alice. When her daughter didn't look up, she turned to Reggie.

'This is the most ridiculous thing I've ever heard. Totally ridiculous.'

'Why don't you wait to hear from Natalie,' Reggie tried to help.

'Is she pregnant?' Frustrated that Alice still hadn't looked up, Veronica tapped her daughter's leg with her foot.

'No, she's not knocked up,' Alice said. 'She just wants to get married.'

'That's the most ridiculous thing...'

'You said that.'

'She'd be throwing her life away. It's her second year at university. She's got her whole life to live and yet the first guy she sleeps with she wants to marry.'

'How do you know it's the first guy?' Alice released herself from her torture, rolled over onto her back and tucked in her knees.

'Why aren't you being more helpful. You could talk her out of it.'

'Sounds like you'll try to. What's the point?'

Veronica looked at her daughter with venom. 'This is not a joke.' She felt tears in her eyes.

'Speak to her yourself, I've got to rehearse.'

Reggie, relieved at an excuse to get out of the kitchen and escape this conversation, stood up quickly. The two went to the piano in the other room and pretty soon Veronica could hear

Alice's weedy voice attempting 'If They Could See Me Now'.

Veronica tried to call Natalie but the phone in her dorm rang and rang unanswered. Frustrated and sick to death of Alice and Reggie and the lot of them, she put the dog on its lead and marched out to the park.

Fang was a Yorkshire terrier, with fur shaved to look like a teddy bear and a red ribbon in his fringe to hold a little fountain of hair out of his beady eyes. Despite his toy-like appearance, he was fearless and as soon as Veronica let him off his lead he dashed over to worry some bigger dogs, yapping up at them and balancing on his back legs to snap at their necks. When the dogs' owners looked over and tutted, Veronica put Fang on his lead and dragged him away.

She tugged at his collar a little too fiercely and walked a little too fast, so the dog had to trot along uncomfortably to keep up with her. Veronica felt she'd been ambushed by Natalie. She had invited a whole gang of people to lunch that Sunday and Natalie knew that it would be a full house when she made her announcement. Bruce, Reggie and Bunny would be there, so it would be impossible for Veronica to make a scene. Oh, she could just imagine Bunny's patronising response. Whether she approved or didn't approve, there would be something she'd say to point out that this was Veronica's fault. Something in the way she'd brought up her children had led to this. If only Bobbi were still alive. She'd be the one to ask how to deal with it.

As she thought of her old friend, who had been dead now over ten years, Veronica started to sniff. If Bobbi were alive, she would read her palm and tell her it was all going to work out. She would look into the auras of everyone at the dinner table and see right through them. She'd encourage Veronica not to be afraid of her emotions and to harness her feelings for use in her singing. Bobbi had always had faith in Veronica, telling her that everything experienced contributed to a better performance. It had been Alan who had invited Bobbi to Australia to design costumes for the Adelaide theatre and supposedly keep a home-sick Veronica happy. Bobbi had jumped at the chance to get out of cold drab England for a few months. Not once did Alan say he felt responsible after Bobbi had drowned, but Bobbi would never have been in Adelaide if Alan hadn't invited her; still, Veronica had never heard him utter a word of remorse. Veronica had started making plans to return to London straight after Bobbi's funeral, and Alan hadn't tried to convince her otherwise. At the time they'd said the appropriate things about how they were going to miss each other, but it had been a relief then to be apart.

Thinking of Alan made her angry again. She took Fang off his lead and sat down on a park bench to calm herself. They'd had plans to be a great artistic couple, but she had to admit that it could never have happened. Not once they had their kids and she was stuck with that burden. How could she be expected to focus on her craft when she had all this responsibility? She'd had one hand tied behind her back since Natalie was born. And now her eldest daughter was talking about getting married herself?! Veronica shook her head. The girl was kidding herself if she thought she could have what she wanted once she went down that path. She'd be pregnant soon and then might as well consider her career and her life over. And how would it look to everyone that, in this day and age, when people were living together with no fuss, she had turned out to be so traditional, so ordinary? Veronica thought again of the upcoming Sunday lunch. Bruce would put in his two-penneth, she could rely on that. He never shied away from chipping in a comment about the kids. Alice would probably be moody because she'd not be the centre of attention. And Reggie would just sit there being pretty as Bunny pontificated. To hell with them all, Veronica thought. What right did they have to judge her? She called over the little dog and stood. She was going to put on her best front, be so convincing that this was water off a duck's back that nobody would see how much it upset her. It would be just a happy Sunday lunch. Maybe she'd even get her hair done. Let them all enjoy the drama, but none of them was going to have one up on her. If there was one thing Veronica knew, it was how to put on an act. She'd come to realise that if you put on a good enough show you could find yourself actually believing it.

VIII

Fish pie, green beans and baked apples. Or maybe fish pie, peas and apricot crumble. Veronica was up early and staring into her open fridge like she was reading an oracle, looking for answers, as if getting the menu right for this disaster-waiting-to-happen Sunday lunch could save her from the agony that was sure to unfold. She was already dressed, the house was clean, and Fang had been dragged up and down the street to do 'his business'. She had two hours before Bruce, Bunny, Reggie and Natalie arrived, probably in that order. She'd found out a little from Alice about the boy Natalie was bringing to lunch. A New Yorker, from Brooklyn, who Natalie had met on holiday last year in Amsterdam. He was called Sal and worked for his father's business, which had something to do with importing olive oil. Fish pie, peas and upside-down pudding. Decision made. Veronica gathered up the ingredients for the cake and let the fridge door slap shut.

Italians say that you can taste the love that's gone into the food you cook. Veronica, grinding her teeth as she smacked butter into the flour and sugar, poured in her frustration, her trepidation and her resentment for the judgement she was going to face from her guests. She tutted at the audacity of the girl, when so much had changed for women over the last three decades, when the world was at her feet, yet here she was ready to become a happy little housewife.

Fang stood beside her, looking up, hoping for scraps. Veronica threw him a sliver of pineapple which he sniffed and ignored.

'No one could say I was a bad mother,' she said to the dog. Fang wagged his tail and Veronica bent down to stroke his head.

Bruce arrived first, stepping into the kitchen and inspecting the food that had been prepared.

'I'll keep an eye on this,' he said. 'Why don't you go and put some makeup on. I'll make us both a vodka and tonic.'

'I've got makeup on,' Veronica protested.

'Well a little more colour wouldn't hurt.' Bruce shuffled her out of the kitchen.

Veronica was at her dressing-table staring at her worn-out face when Alice entered. Just out of bed, Alice was still wearing the massive 'Choose Life' T-shirt that she usually slept in, her fashionably permed hair flattened on one side from a good night's sleep.

'Mum, do I have to stay for lunch? It's just that… '

'Yes, you have to stay.'

'A couple of my pals are busking in Covent Garden today and I said I'd join them.'

'I need you here today.' Veronica patted her painted lips with a tissue and stared down her daughter through the mirror.

'Why are you making this such a big deal?' her daughter huffed and left.

Veronica lingered in her bedroom a while and, when she finally returned to the kitchen, Bunny had arrived and was drinking her vodka and tonic and Reggie was on his way upstairs.

Reggie brought flowers, which he arranged in a jug and placed in the centre of the table.

'No, no, no,' said Bunny lifting the flowers and removing them to the sideboard behind her. 'No one can see a thing.'

'V.A.T. for you?' Bruce asked, brandishing the vodka bottle. A nod between the two friends and Bruce poured Reggie a double.

Alice slunk in eventually. She had changed into a dress and scraped her hair back into a ponytail.

'You look presentable,' her grandmother said as the girl leaned down to peck at her cheek.

'Mercy buckets,' Alice chirped and sat. The girl had a sparkling look in her eyes as if she was waiting excitedly for the drama to begin. Veronica put on a wide smile. She was determined that no one would see the state she was in.

When they heard the key in the door, conversation stopped and they all looked towards the corridor. Natalie entered holding Sal's hand. He was shorter than Veronica had imagined, a dark-skinned blue-eyed man who looked far too old for her daughter and was wearing high-waisted acid-washed jeans that bulged like clown trousers and a waistcoat over a t-shirt.

'Mum, this is Sal.'

They shook hands and Veronica introduced the people around the table.

'Sal?' said Bunny. 'Is that short for something?'

'Salvatore,' he answered. 'I'm named after my great uncle and my mom's step-father.'

'Is that the same person?' Bruce asked.

'Yes, sir, it is.' Sal was still standing. Veronica realised that there were not enough chairs and asked her youngest daughter to go and get the piano stool.

'She can do it,' Alice said. 'I'm tucked in here.'

Once they were seated, Bruce started the interrogation.

'How long are you in the UK?'

'I'm here for 11 days, sir,' said Sal, all eyes on him.

'Oh, please don't call me sir,' Bruce scoffed.

'What would you prefer?' Alice piped up, 'Ma'am?'

The questioning continued with Bruce as key inquisitor, Bunny following up for additional insight and Reggie smiling inanely and nodding at everything, including the questions. Sal was 30, a full eleven years older than Natalie. His mother had been born in Sicily and gone to live in the U.S. with his grandmother when she was a child. He didn't speak Italian. He had always planned to visit Sicily but hadn't managed it yet.

'Maybe you could go for your honeymoon,' said Alice. Before anything further could be said on the dreaded subject of marriage, Veronica made a big fuss of taking the pie out of the oven and serving up big scoops of the sloppy dish onto everyone's plate.

'This looks delicious,' said Sal, scooping his fork into the mush before Veronica had even sat back down.

'Sal's mother is a wonderful cook too,' said Natalie, stroking her boyfriend's arm. 'I haven't met her yet, but she's going to teach me all the old family recipes.'

'My grandmother too,' Sal added, his mouth full of food. 'She's a great cook. Peasant food, you know?'

'Is that why you eat like a peasant?' said Bunny. Sal turned to look at her, but his face didn't register any discomfort.

'My grandma is one hell of a character,' he continued. 'She's the one who can cook up a great meal. Well, she's in a nursing home now, so she doesn't do much cooking. But she keeps herself busy arguing with the nursing staff and putting curses on the other residents.'

'How droll,' Bunny sniffed, holding up her empty vodka and tonic glass and giving the ice cubes a rattle to signal for another drink.

The conversation ebbed between Sal's impressions of the UK as it compared to USA – he was very complimentary and polite – and more probing questions about his background.

'You took over your father's business?' Bruce spoke like a barrister. 'Is that because he retired?'

'Disappeared,' said Sal nonchalantly.

'It's a sad story,' Natalie said. 'One day he just disappeared.'

'Bit like our dad,' said Alice.

Bunny was horrified. 'Your father did not disappear.'

Veronica stepped in. 'Alice, are you just going to sit there chipping in these bitchy little comments all day?'

Alice smiled and looked down. 'I'm on a roll,' she muttered.

Sal and Reggie had second helpings. Bruce left his food almost untouched, swigging wine instead and leaning back in his chair until it creaked. As the conversation stumbled awkwardly on, Veronica watched Natalie. Her daughter had a foolish smile on her face, not unlike the one she was sure was plastered on her own.

Natalie told them that she was taking Sal down to visit her

brother at his boarding school. She'd spoken to Alex on the phone and he was competing in a fencing tournament that they could go and watch. Bruce registered his disappointment that the boy had chosen fencing over something like rugby or football.

'You couldn't be more wrong,' said Bunny. 'Fencing is the sport of kings.'

'And a few queens.' Bruce was quick with his response. 'I was just hoping that we could butch the boy up a little.'

'There is nothing wrong with my grandson,' said Bunny, shaking her glass again. Veronica just moved the bottle of vodka onto the table in front of her. Bunny didn't seem to need the tonic at this point.

'Reggie is American,' Natalie declared helpfully. Reggie, who had stayed silent for most of the meal, looked a little surprised and did a wave.

'I sure am,' he said. 'East coast.'

'Yeah, I go east sometimes for my work,' said Sal. 'Where you from?'

'Here, there, nowhere.' Reggie stood to clear the plates. 'What about this dessert we've been promised?'

The upside-down pudding was stuck to the bottom of the pan and, despite tapping it with the enthusiasm of a kid making a sandcastle, Veronica was forced to give up and spoon it into bowls directly from the tin. An upside-down, upside-down cake. No one seemed to notice because Bunny had brought them to the inevitable conversation and asked about the engagement.

The plan was set out by Natalie as she poked at her dried-up pudding. She was going to finish university, then go to live in New York with Sal. They'd be married, and she'd be able to work once she got her green card, which should take about six months.

'I don't think it's a good idea,' said Veronica. She was slurring her words and it surprised her. She must have had more to drink than she realised. 'Can you imagine what people will say? What will I say when they ask what's happened to Natalie?'

'You'll say I got married. Anyway, who's asking you about me?'

'You're way too young. What's the rush?'

'I need my green card,' Natalie argued.

'I wish I could get a green card,' said Alice. 'Then I could work on Broadway. I think you're lucky to be going to live in America. Escaping this place. I'd love to get out of England.'

'You're going on a cruise,' said Natalie.

'Yes, but only for eight weeks.'

'Well,' Veronica stood. 'If you're lucky the ship will sink.' There was silence.

Eventually Bunny suggested that Reggie play something 'nice' and they take coffees in the other room. Bunny led the way, taking her glass and tucking the almost empty bottle of vodka under her arm. Reggie followed carrying the piano stool that Sal had vacated.

In the kitchen, Veronica struggled with the percolator, ripping the coffee filter so that coffee spilled into the jug below. She could hear Reggie playing and Bunny singing, *'Sally, Sally, pride of our alley...'*

'Oh, for fuck's sake,' she said. Bruce got up slowly and went over to help.

Bunny rarely sang. She must have been really pissed, Veronica thought. Not exactly tuneless but husky and deep, she barked through the chorus. *'Salleee...'*

'Mum,' Natalie kept her voice calm. 'I know this is a shock, but it doesn't have to be such a bad thing. I'm not going to give up my career.'

Veronica didn't want to talk about it. Instead she went through to the entrance hall towards the music. Bunny was leaning against the mantlepiece, the painting of the two girls behind her, the now empty bottle balanced precariously on the edge of the shelf.

As Reggie continued playing, Bunny moved over to Veronica and in a stage-whisper said, 'I know there's a certain appeal about these rough types; God knows I've bedded my fair share of thugs, but they're not who you marry. I'll have a word with her.'

'You will?'

'I'll tell her that, although we all appreciate that she's mature, she shouldn't jump into the first marriage that comes along. And you'd be lost without her. She holds everything together in this family and her brother and sister would just lose the plot if she wasn't around.'

The doorbell rang.

Veronica opened the door to Dawn. She was back from her holiday and she'd left Eileen downstairs to bring up the bags because she was desperate to see the dog. She called his name. When Fang did not materialise, Veronica had no choice but to invite Dawn in to look for him.

Fang was sitting in the kitchen in front of Sal who was giving him instructions in booming New Yorkese.

'I've been called a dog whisperer,' he was saying, giving a hand gesture that the dog ignored.

Dawn swept down to floor level and disrupted the lesson, pulling Fang into her arms and snuggling her face into his fur.

'I've had Dobermans for the last few years. The most intelligent breed,' Sal said. 'And loyal. Those dogs would do anything for you.'

'Fang has a mind of his own,' said Dawn. She stood up and introduced herself to Sal. When he announced himself as Natalie's fiancé, she didn't show any surprise. She smiled at everyone, apologised for the interruption and picked up her dog. Veronica walked her out.

As they moved through the entrance hall, Dawn held up her dog's tiny paw and made him wave at Reggie and Bunny who were now sitting side by side on the same piano stool.

'Quick word,' Dawn said as she stepped out of the door and Veronica followed her into the corridor, pulling the door half shut behind her.

'You know that American bloke?' she said.

'Just met him today. I know absolutely nothing about him.'

'I think he's a villain. That's my professional opinion.'

'You only spoke to him for two seconds.'

'There are some things that don't take more than two seconds and spotting a criminal is one of them,' said Dawn, then she laughed. 'Call it a sixth-sense. I should work for MI5. You tell Natalie to keep her eyes open.'

Veronica came back into the flat, although the temptation to stay outside was agonising. Bruce had made coffee and Reggie and Bunny were back in the kitchen. Bunny was standing but leaning against a wall, coffee splashing as she waved her cup in time with her lecture.

'I, myself, am a widow. But not everyone is that lucky. Not everyone gets one marriage. You have to choose very wisely. Of course, there's nothing wrong with getting married a few times if that's what it takes. My son is onto his third wife.' Bunny stopped talking, realising she had probably overstepped a mark that even she recognised.

'Alan's married again?' Veronica asked.

After waiting for long enough to see that her silent mother wasn't going to faint, Natalie stood up and walked over to put her arm around Veronica, who was rooted to the spot, staring at Bunny.

'Mum, we didn't tell you because we didn't want you to be upset.'

'You knew?'

'They were bridesmaids,' said Bunny. Then she slapped her own hand over her mouth and went to sit down. It was the first time that Veronica had seen her repentant about something she'd said. But there was no pleasure in it for her.

'I suppose your brother...'

'Alex and John split the best man role,' said Alice. 'We didn't mean to hurt you, Mum. We just decided to keep it quiet.'

Veronica shrugged off her daughter's comforting arm and glared at her.

'OK,' Bruce stood. 'Everyone out. Lunch is over.'

Only Reggie got up to leave. 'Not you,' said Bruce. 'You kids take your grandmother home. Salvatore go with them. We've met you now, job done.'

Sal reached out his hand and thanked Veronica for a lovely lunch. She didn't reach back.

It took the group about ten minutes to gather up their stuff and stagger out the door, amid protests.

Sal was trying to be diplomatic. 'It's not a problem. I know what families are like.'

'Not this family you don't,' snapped Veronica. 'You do not know what my family is like.' He smiled again, re-buttoned the waistcoat that he'd opened to accommodate the large meal and left the room.

'Oh, Mum,' said Natalie, following him out.

'No one could say I was a bad mother,' Veronica called out after them.

NATALIE

I

Natalie seemed to be the only one watching the safety demonstration. She wasn't scared of flying but she was fascinated by the casual way the airline staff alluded to the possible death of hundreds of passengers with their smiles and well-rehearsed hand gestures. They synchronised their moves like backing singers. The air hostess in front of her pointed to a plastic whistle on the rubber life jacket around her neck as if it was a key piece of life-saving equipment. Natalie almost smiled. If you're in the sea struggling to stay afloat, you wouldn't have the breath to blow into a whistle and the sound would be lost in the crashing waves. It was an unconvincing scenario, like watching a badly written play performed by the shittiest actors. She gave up and joined the rest of the business people, holiday makers and families staring out the window and poking around in the pouch in front of her while she waited for the plane to take off.

She should have been more excited. She was going to live in America, going to get married. It's true that the argument with her mother and Bruce had soured the big farewell but fuck them, this was her life and she had to stop putting them first at some point. The plastic wall beside her shuddered as the plane's wheels left the runway. The aircraft itself felt like a stage set to Natalie. It wasn't difficult to imagine what was behind the moulded yellow walls, the chaotic reality of wires and steel, covered over by a cheery plastic casing designed to make everyone inside feel at ease. It was an illusion that seemed to be working. People were chatting and smiling at each other.

When the electronic beep signalled that passengers could undo their safety belts, there was a communal murmur of relief as if everyone had been told that the fun could really start. What children.

Natalie couldn't concentrate on the book she held in her hand and the film wasn't due to start for another fifteen minutes. Maybe she should go to the back of the plane and have a cigarette? She could already smell sweet tobacco smoke drifting up the aisle. Others must have had the same idea. She counted up the ciggies in her pack and did a calculation based on the number of hours 'til she landed. No, she'd leave it for now, wait until she got really desperate.

When she had first gone to university, Natalie had had the same feeling that she had now, of escape; the anticipation of being free of the chaos of her family, relieved of the weight of looking after everything because her mother was so often distracted. Veronica made decisions based on knee-jerk reactions that rarely worked out perfectly for herself or the rest of them. Natalie's distance didn't keep her free for long, however. Family responsibilities crept into her university life and by the third year she had found herself arranging care for her grandmother in Sheffield, chasing her father for money to pay her brother's school fees and acting as go-between when Alice had one of her tantrums and fell out with their mother.

Natalie had always been the reliable one, and she was sick of it. She'd put in more than enough effort through the years. It's not that people ever asked for her help explicitly, but it went without saying that if Natalie didn't step in things just wouldn't get done. Natalie wondered if she'd ever felt differently. Maybe when she was really, really young, maybe before her little brother was born, maybe then she had enjoyed a feeling of being looked after. She couldn't put her finger on exactly when that had changed but it was a long time ago, so long ago that it had been well and truly her responsibility to hold things together after the drowning accident, when her father freaked out, her mother went silent and her brother and sister just couldn't understand.

But things were going to be different this time. Veronica had given her eldest daughter an ultimatum. If Natalie decided to marry Sal, she'd never speak to her again. It was such a grand announcement, made with Bruce as a witness, that as soon as it was said both women knew the damage had been done. Natalie didn't get a good bye. She'd packed her things over the next few days in an atmosphere of simmering fury. When the time came to exit, her mother was at her dressing-table putting her curlers in and refused to catch her eye. Natalie left her keys on the kitchen table and struggled with her suitcases out the door. Her breath caught in her throat as she tried to take in what was happening. She was going to be free from all this drama. She'd miss her brother and sister, but she could do with a break from her mother and her crazy friends. She put down her suitcases to zip up her coat. Perhaps this is what it felt like to be let out of prison. It was probably why most of the TV footage she'd seen of prisoners walking free showed them looking bewildered and frightened. She picked up her suitcases and steadied herself.
'Oh shit,' she said.

Sal was there to meet her at the airport, waiting outside the terminal, as arranged. He was standing beside a white sports car, talking with a policeman, and didn't stop his conversation when he saw her, just looked up and waved. She dropped the cases besides the car and waited for him to turn around. When he did, it was as if he'd just spotted her, reaching over to grab her in his arms enthusiastically, smacking kisses over her face and neck and slapping her bum.

'She's here at last,' he said to no one and everyone. 'My English Rose.'

Only one suitcase fit in the trunk of the car, so they squeezed the second into an almost non-existent back seat and set off. The city was hot and, despite heavy traffic slowing them to a crawl, Sal revved the engine and blasted music as if they were racing along an open road.

'I can't wait to get back to your place,' Natalie shouted over a guitar solo, 'I could do with a shower. It's a hell of a trip.'

'Right you are, princess,' Sal smiled over at her. 'Just a quick stop and then we'll get you straight home.'

Natalie had been to New York twice since she'd met Sal but seeing it now as her new home felt exciting and not quite real. The sun setting on the skyscraper horizon, the yellow cabs cutting in front, the billboards promising everything from strippers to personal injury lawyers – it was a different world.

By the time they made it over the bridge to Manhattan the sun had set, and Natalie was getting hungry. Sal drove erratically, yelling at other drivers and revving at red lights, eager to get to his destination. He was strumming his hands on the steering wheel and biting his lips. 'Oh yes, oh yes,' he kept saying.

It took thirty minutes to get downtown to Alphabet City. Natalie looked out the window feeling uneasy. Sal hadn't spoken to her for a while. She didn't want to start a fight or be a pain in the arse on her first night.

'Should we stop for something to eat?' she suggested.

'Sorry, sweetheart, won't be long, I promise.' He thumped on the horn to move a van in front that was taking too long after the light turned green. The streets were darker than those big New York avenues and people were sitting on the sidewalk in front of shops and apartment blocks or huddled together on the corners. All of them seemed to be watching the cars.

Sal pulled over to a curb. 'Natalie, I just need you to sit in the back for a bit. Won't take any time at all and then I'll have you home I promise.' He waited for her to get out, looking at her and smiling.

'It looks dangerous around here,' she said, not moving.

'You're with me, baby. Don't you worry.' Seeing that she wasn't getting out, Sal opened his own door and went around the front of the car. He opened the door on her side and held out his hand. His gesture was almost galante. He flipped back the seat, squashed the suitcase down into the footwell and helped her in. 'Ten minutes tops.'

With Natalie in back, peaking over the passenger seat, Sal

drove off. After a couple of blocks, he pulled once again to the curb and waved to a small guy, who walked over with a little skip in his step.

'You got an eight?' Sal said, and the guy nodded and smiled. He leaned down further so he could see into the back of the car, looking directly at Natalie. He winked.

'That your kid?' the guy said to Sal.

'Get in,' said Sal and the man did his little dance-walk around the front of the car to the passenger side.

Once the guy was inside, Sal drove down the block and took a turn. With a gesture from the guy that made sense to Sal, he pulled over and backed into an alley. The guy got out.

'Do you know that man?' Natalie asked as they waited.

'Honey, I just asked you to be quiet for a bit, right?' Sal was alternating between staring out the window and checking in the rear-view mirror. 'We're almost done and then I'm all yours. I've got you a little treat when we get home. I suppose this is just a little treat for me.'

The guy returned, leaned into Sal's window and shook his hand. Sal grasped the guy's hand in both of his as if he was a long-lost friend. 'Cool, cool,' he said. The guy turned away and Sal drove off.

'Let's get out of here and then I'll let you back in the front.' Sal was driving and with his other hand poking around in the well between the two seats for a biro. At the next light, he took the pen and dipped his head down, snorting at something he held low in his lap. He sat up and turned the radio loud.

'Let's get you home. I am so excited to have you here. I've got all sorts planned for you, baby. We're going to Mom's tomorrow for lunch. She's really looking forward to meeting you again. And then I want to take you to see the sights. Go do a little shopping. Anything you want.'

Sal continued talking excitedly, especially after Natalie had been repositioned back in the front of the car. He got a bit teary-eyed at one point saying how much he loved her and that he knew he was the luckiest guy in the world. He was so silly that

Natalie started to giggle at him.

'You big softie,' she said.

'*Black velvet* … ' he sang along to the radio, looking over to her and pursing his lips.

'Keep your eyes on the road,' she laughed.

It must have been the middle of the night, but Natalie was wide awake. Sal wasn't in bed beside her. They'd had a great evening, feasted on a meal he'd prepared, made love. He'd offered her cocaine, but she'd declined. They'd had a bottle of wine and then fallen asleep. Now it was dark, and she could hear the sound of TV in the other room. Natalie got up and stooped down to get a T-shirt that Sal had slung on the chair. She checked herself in the mirror and tucked her hair behind her ears before going into the living room.

Sal was on the couch in sweatpants. He flashed her a look and smiled before turning his gaze back to the TV. On screen was a noisy ad with bright images of girls looking urgently into the camera with a phone number flashing up beside them and a string of credit card logos across the top. Sal patted the sofa beside him and Natalie sat down. He was sweaty, and the leather couch squeaked as he leaned forward to take another line of coke from a dinner plate on the low table in front of him.

Natalie took a cigarette out of a half-empty pack and lit it. She looked around the room. It wasn't exactly stylish. The leather couch, the TV, the table. Everything was practical but there wasn't a picture on the wall. Her family home had been a riot of colour and chaos, usually a mess, with bookcases spilling over with novels, records and unopened letters, too many pots and pans crowding the kitchen counter and usually a sink fully of dirty dishes. Sal's place was immaculate, empty even. There were grey vertical blinds at the window which, even when closed, let in slivers of light from the streetlamp outside and made the room look like a prison cell.

'How do you feel about redecorating?' she asked.

He laughed and nudged her. 'You saying I don't have good

taste?'

'It's a bit sparse in here.'

'Yeah, I never got 'round to making it look good. You choose what you like. I want you to feel like this is your home too.'

They sat for a while staring at the TV which just seemed to be broadcasting one ad after another. Natalie wasn't tired, but she was getting bored of sitting there in the dark being yelled at by voiceovers warning about the dangers of not having a funeral plan, or recommending a new product to get buns of steel.

'Alright, let me have a line,' she said, and Sal looked at her with a smile.

'You done this before?'

'At a party,' she picked up the hollowed-out biro, 'but it didn't have any effect.'

He laughed and watched her amateur attempt to snort the cocaine.

Only a couple of minutes later and they were both buzzing, laughing at the TV screen, mocking an action film that was impossible to follow, and kissing each other. When the phone rang with Sal's mother asking what time they were coming around, they realized it was morning.

Angela lived in Queens. She'd moved there to be nearer her mother's nursing home, which she visited every other day. Her apartment was in the basement of a family home; it had its own entrance and a little patch of yard where she could sit with coffee and a cigarette or hang out washing on a sunny day. She opened the door seconds after they rang the bell and smiled up at Natalie.

'I forget what a tall girl you are,' she said. She reached forward and hugged Natalie to her, ignoring her son, who moved passed them and into the apartment with the boxed pie they'd bought on the way.

'What a beautiful dress.' Angela led her future daughter-in-law inside. 'You look so pretty, no one would believe you'd just travelled across the world.'

'It's lovely to see you again,' Natalie replied.

'Oh, the way you talk,' Angela said. 'Straight outta a movie.'

Inside, the apartment was cheery and welcoming. Photos of the family were in frames on the walls; colourful plants, perfectly artificial, were lined up along a shelf and a painting of a young woman in a see-through negligee and perky breasts hung behind a large sofa that had a fitted plastic cover and, to further protect it, crocheted doilies across each arm.

'Ma, we got ya coconut pie,' Sal said, coming in from the kitchen and sitting on the sofa, which squeaked. 'Natalie has never tried a coconut pie.'

Angela laughed. 'Never tried coconut pie? Well, you are in for a treat. I'll bet you'll be trying a whole load of new things now you're living here.'

'Yeah, you can say that.' Sal looked over to Natalie as if they had an in-joke. She half-frowned back at him.

'I've got soda, perhaps a beer for you, Sal.' Angela was plumping up an already plumped cushion on a recliner chair, and she invited Natalie to sit in it so grandly it was like she was leading her to a throne. 'And for Natalie I even bought English tea. Real English tea. I got lemon and milk, that's right, isn't it?'

Natalie was charmed. 'I'd love a cup of tea. How kind of you.'

Angela hurried off to the kitchen and Natalie could hear her trying out the English accent on herself, 'how kind of you.'

Sal stood up and went to the cabinet by the window.

'What you got at the moment?' he said, opening the doors.

'Take a look yourself,' Angela called from the kitchen. 'I've got some beautiful dress shirts, a couple of those leather waist bags that you see everyone wearing, and... ' Her voice faded away.

Sal rifled through the shelves and retrieved a small box. It was an electronic organizer, the type that you could use to store all the details from your address book and would give you reminders about your meetings and appointments. When Angela returned to the living room, Sal asked her how much she wanted for it.

'Have it, Sal,' Angela said. 'If you know anyone who wants one, let me know.'

After a cup of tea, they sat down to lunch at the kitchen table. Angela uncovered a steaming lasagne that was on the kitchen counter and served up a brick-size wedge to both Natalie and Sal. The portion she gave herself was only enough for a couple of mouthfuls. Angela was a tiny woman, so thin that her elbows stuck out like her arms were branches of a pruned tree. She had skin the colour of a strong white coffee and big brown eyes that she'd drawn around with eyeliner to make them even more striking. She was glamorous. Angela picked at her food with her fork and chatted with Natalie, asking her questions about London, and explaining the food she'd cooked in the minutest detail.

'I don't skin the tomatoes,' she confessed. 'It's not that I can't be bothered, I just hate when they go into a mush. You know what I'm talking about?'

'I can well imagine.' Natalie noticed herself getting more English with her every response. She saw how much Angela was enjoying her accent and couldn't help playing up to the image she saw reflected in her soon-to-be mother-in-law's eyes. The proper English lady.

Natalie had been told by Sal how much food meant to Angela and she asked for a second helping, not just because the food was delicious but to show her appreciation. Once finished, though, Angela didn't clear away the plates but instead took a dish of salt cod out of the oven, removed tea towels to reveal two plates of vegetables that she'd prepared and put some large squares of bread on a plate for them to share. With difficulty, because she was full to the point of feeling queasy, Natalie ate through the cod, some eye-wateringly bitter broccoli rabe, and buttery sweet potato. She did her best but at the end confessed that the coconut pie would have to wait for another day.

Sal looked over at her smiling. 'You gotta pace yourself, baby. Ma really knows how to cook.'

Angela made them all a strong coffee.

Natalie got up to use the bathroom and Angela insisted on showing her the way, although it was just by the front door. She wanted a private word with her and, before Natalie went in, Angela leaned forward and said, 'Sal told me your family was very nice and I really want you to feel as welcome here.'

'I'm not so sure they were as friendly as they could have been.'

Angela reached up and patted Natalie's cheek. 'You'll meet the rest of the family soon and I want you to know everyone's very excited about the wedding. You're just what this family needs.'

Natalie stood with one hand on the bathroom door handle waiting for Angela to finish talking. When she paused just long enough, Natalie nodded and went inside.

The wedding. Yes, that was something she should be focusing on. She had never been one of those girls who fantasised about wedding dresses or their life as a missus. In fact, she didn't know anyone who was like that. But she did love Sal, he was different from anyone she'd ever met. He didn't seem scared of anything, didn't kowtow to anyone and, when she was with him, she didn't have to feel in charge. She could get looked after for a change.

When she returned to the kitchen, Angela stopped talking abruptly and smiled at her.

'Carry on, Ma,' said Sal, 'you can say anything in front of Natalie that you can say to me.'

Angela paused for a second and then continued. 'I've just been wondering why there haven't been any deliveries for over a week. There must be something going on.'

'They've cut me off,' Sal said.

'What do you mean? What did you do, Salvatore?'

'Nothing, I don't know, you know what he's like. He's upset about something and he's letting me suffer for a while.'

'Do you want me to talk to him?'

'Fuck, Ma, no. It's bad enough… ' Then they were both silent for a bit.

'Well, get this straightened out. I don't want to get involved but I won't be able to stop myself if you're messing this up for everyone.'

'Leave me alone, Ma,' Sal whined. 'I know what I'm doing.'

'I just hope you do.'

Natalie didn't know where to look and stirred her coffee seriously.

Despite the large meal, Sal still had a slice of pie, another coffee and then asked his mother to pack up food for them to take with them.

'What are you two doing this afternoon?' Angela asked as she showed them to the door.

'I'm going to sleep, Ma, I'm exhausted,' said Sal. 'I'm not sleeping well at all. I was up most of the night.'

Angela looked at him with concern, then reached into the pocket of the apron that was hanging by the door with the coats. She pulled out a little pack of pills. 'Here, try these. Start off with a couple. Don't overdo it.'

'Thanks for lunch, Ma,' Sal bent down and gave his mother a kiss on the cheek. Natalie followed his example and they left. As they walked up the stairs back to ground level, they could hear Angela bolting the door with multiple locks and muttering to herself in Italian.

In the car on the way home, Natalie sang Angela's praises. After all that had happened with her own mother in the last few months, it was great to have a warm family to rely on.

The car sped along the expressway back to Brooklyn with the windows down and muggy air blowing in to keep them awake.

'She did seem a bit worried about you,' Natalie said, still with her head half hanging out of the window.

'Well, the men don't last long in our family.' Sal laughed, and even more so when he saw how shocked Natalie looked. 'No, no,' he kept chuckling. 'Nothing for you to worry about. I ain't going nowhere.'

'What happened to your Dad?'

'It's a long story,' said Sal.

'Yeah, but it would be good for me to know. It's going to be my family too, right?' She gave him a winning smile.

'We gotta get home. Need to let the dog out into the yard. And, anyway, there's not much to tell. My Dad, Buddy, was working for a guy who was involved in a bit of shady stuff. When I was about 12 or 13, he was mixed up in some gang payback; one day he was there, next he was gone.'

'Maybe, he's still alive?'

Sal looked at her incredulously. Then he laughed again. 'Grandma, she's the one to watch. Sweet little old lady? No, she ain't.'

'The lady I met last time I visited?'

'Yeah, Grandma. That old woman has balls on her.'

He was silent for a bit, humming along to a tune on the radio. Natalie became frustrated.

'Tell me.'

'What's to tell? She was working with Buddy when he disappeared. It was a big old deal. Some people came to get her too, but she outsmarted them. Hid and took any incriminating evidence out of the apartment.'

'She's brave.'

'Yeah, you could say that. The man my Dad worked for was pretty damn relieved. She didn't spill anything to the cops either. They picked her up in the park, all confused, you know? Yeah, right? I think she knew exactly what was going on. Anyway, the guy, my Dad's boss, he put her in the best old folks' home around here. She's living like a queen.'

'That's nice of him.'

'Yeah,' Sal smiled patronisingly as he said it. 'Nice.'

'It's all new to me,' Natalie stuck her face out of the window again.

'Let's get home, knock back a couple of Mom's sleeping pills and pass out.'

II

The Australian sun burned through the roof of the car and, even with the windows open, it felt like they were being cooked. Natalie's legs stuck to the plastic seat and her towelling beach dress was sweaty already. Mum was driving, with Dad in the passenger seat reading a map, Alice in the way-way back and Natalie, Alexander and their parents' friend Bobbi in the back seat trying to keep clear of each other, so their sticky legs didn't touch.

'It's ten or fifteen minutes from here,' Dad said. 'Unspoilt. It's going to be beautiful.'

Bobbi was playing with her amber necklace like it was a string of worry beads making a rhythmical clicking sound that was comforting. They'd already drunk the juice they'd bought for the journey, and they'd promised not to break into the picnic until they arrived.

Natalie watched her father through the rear-view mirror. Having folded the map on his knee he was staring ahead. It was difficult to see what he was focussing on, but he did often go into a world of his own. Then he winked. Bobbi chuckled. 'Let's see what we can see in the sky,' she said. Natalie knelt on the seat to get a good view of the clouds, Alex leaned over Bobbi and peered upwards.

'A bunny,' Alex said.

'You always see a bunny,' said Alice from the way-way back. 'Can't you be more original?'

'Over there could be a question mark,' said Natalie.

'I see a pretty leaf,' said Bobbi, 'look, just there.'

'It's more like a teardrop,' said Natalie.

'Yes, it is.'

'A dragon,' Alex was excited and pointing. 'There, there, a dragon.'

'That's the same cloud as the bunny,' said Alice.

'A half bunny half dragon,' said Mum. 'That'll put the wind up everyone at Easter.'

130

The beach was empty. Mum laid out the towels and opened the Esky; Dad carried the surfboards down from the road where they'd parked. They were only children's polystyrene versions of the real thing so weren't strong enough to stand on, but it was fun to float on top of the waves and kick your legs. Alice and Natalie took one each. Alex wasn't a good swimmer yet and he stayed on the sand with Mum to dig a trench from the picnic to the water's edge. Bobbi and Dad said that they should swim out for a bit and all race back.

They lost the surfboards very quickly. Just slipped out of their grasp as they tumbled with each wave. They were separated from each other too. Natalie was paddling frantically, but going under, deep, looking up through the water to the sun which shone like a spotlight that she kept heading for every time she was dragged under. She had been taught front crawl at school just a few weeks before but couldn't even try; instead she doggy-paddled and gasped every time her face reached the air before sinking again. At one point when she was so deep she thought she could touch the bottom, she saw Bobbi floating above her, amber beads hanging down and hair covering her face as she flopped to and fro on the surface. Then Natalie saw her mother. Mum grabbed the straps of her swimming costume and pulled her up. Mum was holding Bobbi's swimming costume too and keeping them both at the surface of the water as she kicked her legs towards the shoreline. Natalie tried to help by kicking too. She felt the ground and struggled to get her balance. She could see her little brother standing at the edge of the water watching them and crying. Mum released her grip and Natalie ran up through the shallow water to Alex.

'Where's Dad?' she asked him, her voice a painful whisper.

'He went up there?' Alex wailed, pointing to the path up to the road.

'Alice?'

'I think that's her.' Alex pointed to a string of rocks that formed a jagged semi-circle from the sand into the sea, and

Natalie could see her younger sister, in a little ball, lying on top.

Mum was dragging Bobbi across the shallow stretch of water towards them. She laid her friend down and kissed her fiercely, then pushed on her chest. 'Please, please, please,' she was saying.

Natalie and Alex stood and watched.

Dad had gone to get help. It took him an hour, but he returned with ambulance men. They took over from Mum kissing Bobbi and pushing down on her body. Dad went to bring Alice from the rock to the beach. All three kids stood together away from the adults. Natalie got a towel for each of them and tried to keep them warm.

'When this is all done, we'll get the adults some lovely chocolates, shall we do that?'

'Ice cream?' asked Alex.

'Oh, loads and loads of ice cream,' Natalie promised.

Alice didn't speak. Not at that point or for the next five days.

III

Sal wasn't exaggerating; the nursing home looked like a mansion. New Horizons Residential Home for the Elderly was a grand building in Little Neck with a view of the bay and a circular driveway cut into a manicured lawn. The residents could sit on a strip of green grass by the water and take in the sun each day, catered to by staff in uniforms. It reminded Natalie of a smart hotel. Despite her elegant surroundings, Grandma was vocal about how she hated being watched all the time and how she wished she was back in Brooklyn where her friends were. She sat in a wheelchair in a brown cardigan buttoned up to the neck and with a blanket over her knees. Sal rolled his eyes when she called the place a dump, which didn't go unnoticed by Grandma.

'Perhaps we can go for a walk? It's a lovely day,' said Natalie.

'You go,' said Grandma. 'You can't make me do anything.'

'I didn't mean...'

Sal stood. 'You wanna go back to your room?'

'Yes, get me away from these old people.'

Sal wheeled his grandmother inside and along the corridor. Natalie trailed behind. Grandma ignored the friendly greetings she got from other residents and members of staff. Natalie made up for it with a big grin and a nod of the head to each of them.

Grandma's room was decorated in pale yellow and had pictures on the wall, a crucifix above the bed and a wall-mounted clock that ticked loudly. Natalie noticed a black and white family photo in a frame and went over to inspect it.

'Is this you?' she asked.

'Sal Junior is in there,' said Grandma, cheering up a little. 'I'm the one with the hat.'

Natalie noticed a hole in the photograph, someone had been removed. The body of a man was intact next to a younger Angela but the cardboard from the back was showing through where his head should be. Sal saw her looking and smiled.

Grandma listened to them talk about the upcoming wedding and then asked Sal whether he was still working at the olive oil company or had he started the pizzeria yet.

'I didn't know you wanted to start a pizzeria?' said Natalie.

'I've always wanted to,' he replied. 'Just waiting for the right time. I know someone who says they could help but it's taking too long.'

'What you do...' said Grandma, reaching over to a tea towel that was on the table beside her '...is you wrap up a bit of cloth and put in on your head. Then you can balance the trays.'

Sal laughed. 'They don't do it like that anymore, Grandma.'

It didn't take long for Sal to get bored. He said he was going to go and see if the game was on in the day room. He didn't ask Natalie to go with him.

Natalie made the old lady a cup of coffee and sat with her as she spoke about how she used to make pizza and bread as a kid in Sicily. She said she missed the big village oven that they used to have back in the old country and she'd never tasted anything as good as the bread that came out of it.

She was quiet for a bit and Natalie took the cups to the sink to rinse them.

'Where's Buddy?' Grandma said suddenly.

Natalie was concerned. 'Do you mean Sal? He's just gone to the day room. Do you need him?'

'When I got married it was my father decided who I marry, and I didn't get to say. I wasn't happy about it.' She started chuckling. 'I was not happy.'

'Was that when you married Angela's father?' Natalie asked.

'I was all on my own. Away from my family. I had to join his family and I didn't know them. I hated them.'

'Gosh, that sounds difficult.'

'Now, it's better. Now girls choose. But just because they choose doesn't mean they choose the right ones.'

Grandma was looking tired. Natalie wondered if she should go and find Sal. As if on cue, the door opened and one of the nurses entered. It was time for Grandma to take her medication and then she usually had a nap. Natalie picked up her handbag.

'Angela?' Grandma looked up at Natalie. 'Don't leave me here, Angie?'

'Maybe I should get Sal?' she asked the nurse.

'You leave her with me, honey. She'll be fine.'

Salvatore and Natalie's wedding was not particularly elaborate — they'd only had four months to pull it together — but it was extraordinary. They didn't have a lot of money to splash out on non-essentials. Sal still had his job at the olive oil company and was doing some work on the side for the guy who paid Grandma's bills, but Natalie couldn't earn any money until she had her green card. She did a few shifts at a typing pool that was run by a friend of Sal's family, but it wasn't enough to keep her fully employed. She visited Grandma, spent time with Angela making the wedding arrangements, and hung out with Sal.

Sal was doing coke most nights and, although she tried not

to bug him about it, she did hate how often he was late for work the following day or just didn't show up.

'I'm stressed at the moment,' he'd protest. 'This wedding and everything. Once that's done, this will stop. It's all under control.'

'If we don't have the money for flowers, I don't see how we have money for cocaine,' Natalie argued.

'I don't pay for coke,' he said. 'And please don't worry. This is not physically addictive. This isn't heroin. Not real different from you having a glass of wine each night.'

Natalie tried to call her mother to invite her to the wedding. She spoke to Bruce who said he'd pass on a message but not to expect anything. When she protested, they got into an argument. Bruce was as angry at her as Veronica and said that, if she was insisting on acting the fool, they didn't want to have anything to do with it. Natalie hung up on him. That night, her one glass of wine became a bottle and she took a couple of Angela's sleeping pills as well to relax herself.

'Who is that guy, anyway?' Sal tried to comfort her. 'He isn't your father.'

'I can't really explain it,' she said.

'Well you got me now,' Sal hugged her, lifting her slightly off the ground. 'And I think you're doing exactly the right thing.'

The wedding took place at a large party venue on Long Island called Leo's Palazzo. When Angela had first driven her there, Natalie had thought it was a joke. The big building, visible from the highway, was decorated with sparkly glitter paint, had pillars, fountains and armless statues. Trees shaped into balls on sticks that looked like green ear-buds lined the drive up to the entrance. It was the tackiest thing she'd ever seen. But, as a friend of the family was one of the chefs, they could get a good price on a small room and Natalie saw how much Angela was impressed with the place. She didn't want to say no. Otto, the chef, ran a numbers game to supplement the income he made on the veal escalope and chicken cacciatore he dished up hundreds of times a week. He had shown them to the Caesar Suite, which was a small conference room with a low ceiling and mirrors down all four walls. Angela got teary-eyed as they plotted out where to have the ceremony and when to bring out the buffet. Otto said he'd get them a deal on the booze. Without much input from Sal, it was arranged.

Natalie's side of the family was going to be small. Alice was going to attend, Alan was flying in too. And Reggie, who was in New York anyway, RSVP'd yes.

Natalie met Alice's plane at Newark and they took the bus into Manhattan, chatting excitedly all the way. It was great for the two sisters to be together and Natalie laughed at Alice's stories of life on board the cruise ship and how she'd had to hide from various over-amorous passengers or crew members when they'd had a few drinks.

'I was really tempted to bunk down in one of the lifeboats,' she said. 'You just can't get away from them. Anyone in a skimpy leotard has to spend the whole evening dodging groping hands. I complained to the bursar but fat lot of good that did. I think it's encouraged. The passengers think it's a perk that comes with the price of the ticket.'

They headed straight to Broadway. Alice wanted a photo of herself on the famous street. She pulled a pose in front of The Gershwin Theatre. Natalie felt a twinge of embarrassment, but nobody seemed to bat an eyelid. It was good to show her sister around. Natalie pointed out some of the famous sites as they walked across town to where Alice was staying. It was a pretty ordinary hotel, popular with visitors to conventions, without much to recommend it other than a midtown location and an all-you-can-eat breakfast. The room was small, and the en suite bathroom was in a cupboard separated by a plastic concertina door.

'Let's see what you brought to wear?' Natalie opened her sister's case on the bed. A bottle of gin was on top of her folded clothes along with a plastic beaker with the words 'Celebrity Cruises – get away from it all'.

'Pour us a glass and I'll hang this up,' said Natalie, shaking out the flowery dress that Alice had chosen to bring for the wedding.

Natalie fussed with her sister's unpacking as Alice sat on the floor, sipping gin and bringing her up to speed. She'd been put on the roster for the cruise line, so she'd keep doing that until something better came along. She just wanted to be out of the house. Her mother had gone mad, madder than normal. Bruce wasn't helping. Reggie was perhaps an ally, but he was in New York himself at the moment. Felix De Foe had died, and Reggie had come back to run a Greenwich Village theatre café while he worked out what to do and where to live.

'Mum said he could live with us,' Alice said.

'Poor sod,' said Natalie, rolling her eyes at her sister to mask how guilty she suddenly felt that she wasn't there to sort everything out.

'Reggie wants out of London for a bit. I'm going to see him tomorrow and we'll come together to the wedding. He's borrowed a car.'

'And Dad?'

'His flight arrives tomorrow. He might come straight to the venue.'

Natalie felt a little disappointed. She had imagined that she'd have a little time with her father beforehand, introduce him to Sal, maybe ask him to make a speech or walk her down the aisle or something like that.

'Now, tell me what this wedding is going to be like?' Alice looked up at her mischievously. 'Are there going to be gangsters there?'

'For God's sake don't say anything like that tomorrow.' Natalie was serious. 'Just because they are Sicilians...'

Alice started with a *Godfather* impression and Natalie couldn't help but laugh.

Natalie decided to treat herself to a cab back to Brooklyn. It was getting dark by the time she left her sister's hotel. They were both tipsy and hugged each other dramatically on the street as they parted.

'Are you sure you're doing the right thing?' Alice asked.

'Not you too?' Natalie pulled away from her.

'I'm only trying to be…'

'I'm in it now. Look, I love Sal; we'll work it all out. His family are so kind to me. I need to get this over with, get my green card and then I can start on my career. There's so much I want to do. And Sal's really supportive. It's like having a great big safety net, someone who's looking out for me. It's all going to work out – honestly it is.'

'Yeah, I get it,' Alice sighed and stepped back to let Natalie get in the cab.

'Don't be late,' Natalie said and waved.

Alice was late to the wedding. Reggie and she arrived after the guests had been seated in the rows of white chairs; Sal was standing with his friends and the registrar at the top end of the room, and Natalie was chatting with her father in the corridor waiting to make her entrance. Reggie greeted them, told Natalie she looked beautiful and went in. Alice hugged her sister and father and snuck in too.

It felt strange after so many months in New York to have some of her London family here. It was as if she was being asked to play two different roles at the same time and she wasn't quite sure who to be. Alan was confident and considerate. He'd shaken hands with Sal's family, embraced Sal, offered to walk Natalie down the improvised aisle and agreed to make a speech.

As Natalie and Alan entered, the small crowd swivelled around to smile at them. Alan looked great in a slick suit and baby blue tie. Many of the female guests nodded, nudged each other and promised to introduce themselves to him later. Angela had forewarned them that he was an important theatre director and, although they'd never heard of him, they took her word for it and didn't hide their admiration. Natalie suited her pretty white dress, as all women do, and she caught her own reflection in the mirrored walls and noticed the awkward step by step progress they were making as if they were a pair of wind-up toys.

Natalie looked so young as she stood beside Sal, giving her vows in a clipped English voice, that some of the guests got tears in their eyes. The registrar spoke of the power of love and pronounced her name "Naderlee" which made her want to giggle. Sal was sweating and the intensity of the moment and his expression, like he was up in court, made her want to laugh. Natalie bit her lip and tried to concentrate.

Sal and Natalie had made a tape to play as the two of them walked back through their guests as husband and wife, but the music only got them halfway down the aisle before the tape jammed. Natalie looked over to the waiter who had been charged with pressing "play" and saw him struggling with a spaghetti-tangle of tape. They stopped in the silence for a moment. Then Alan clapped and everyone else did too. Then some cheered and stood up, applauding them until they got to the door, smiling and relieved that it was finally over.

Sal's family, his workmates and a few of the friends that Natalie had made since she'd been in New York mingled with the three people who were there to represent the bride: Alan, being friendly with two women from the hair salon and a nurse from Grandma's residential home; Reggie chatting with Otto who, in chef's uniform, should probably have been in the kitchen but was tucking into canapés and sipping sparkling wine; and Alice, talking to one of the waiters and placing her hand on his arm as she shared her sympathies about working big events. Sal and Natalie held hands as they went around to meet members of the extended family. The men gave Natalie money, which she put in a drawstring bag that Angela had given her before the wedding. Cheques, envelopes with cash, all folded into the bag, which Sal checked periodically to calculate a running total.

When the white chairs had been moved and tables rolled into place, dressed with cloths and laid with cutlery, the guests found seats. Ignoring the name cards that Natalie had asked to be placed according to a well-considered plan, most guests crowded onto a couple of tables near the buffet, while Grandma and her nurse took a table for themselves at the back. Angela said she couldn't eat if you put a gun to her head and so she didn't sit; instead she wandered around the room, talking to everyone and enjoying herself.

Natalie introduced Sal to Reggie.

'Thank you so much for coming,' she said. 'I'm sorry about Felix. Alice told me the news.'

Reggie looked sad for a second. 'It was unexpected,' he said. 'I'm going to be in the States for a while until everything gets sorted. But let's not talk about that, how are you?'

After a bit of catching up, they moved on to talk to someone else. Sal leaned in to whisper to his bride.

'He's a fag, right?' he said.

Natalie was annoyed. 'Don't say that.'

Sal laughed. 'I better tell the guys to stay away from him. Don't want to find themselves alone with him in the bathroom.'

Natalie dropped his hand and walked off. She took herself to Grandma's table.

'Where's your Momma?' Grandma asked Natalie. 'Is your Momma dead?' The nurse, who like all nurses had learned enough from eavesdropping to get the picture, distracted the old lady with food as Natalie made an escape.

Alan gave a speech and, as anticipated, hit the right notes despite knowing little about Sal or his family and not really knowing that much about his own daughter. He added a spattering of Italian which impressed many of the guests and when he asked them to raise their glasses they all did as directed.

Natalie was sitting with Reggie, and Sal had joined a table with some of his pals.

'The tape recorder is broken,' she said. 'It's a bit a quiet.'

'Do you want me to see what I can do?' Reggie stood up.

Reggie left the room and Natalie strolled over to her husband. Sal and his friends were getting boisterous. One of the guys was pinning Sal to a chair with an arm around his neck. They were all laughing.

'You just say the word,' one of Sal's friends said to Natalie, squeezing tighter so that Sal cried out. 'This guy gets out of hand and we'll take care of it for you.'

'Thanks, I suppose,' said Natalie.

'Get the fuck off me,' Sal laughed and broke free. 'I could take you out, all of you.'

'You wouldn't even see us coming,' said another friend.

Then one of the guys stood. 'I want to kiss the bride.' He walked over to Natalie and pulled her towards him.

'Don't you fucking dare,' said Sal, remaining in his seat.

The man had his hands around Natalie's waist and leaned in to kiss her lips, pressing against her mouth for far too long. She pulled back horrified and looked at Sal for assistance.

'You're such a kidder,' Sal said to the guy. Sal didn't look at Natalie, just reached forward to get his beer and took a swig.

There was a commotion by the double doors as they were propped open. Reggie, with the help of Otto and another waiter, was pushing an upright piano into the room. Natalie took the opportunity to move away from the table and towards the piano which they were rolling between the furniture towards the back. Alice came and stood beside her.

'Shall I sing a song?' she asked. Alice didn't wait for an answer, just walked forward to Reggie who had dragged a chair up to the piano.

'Oh god,' said Natalie. She looked around the room for a suitable place to disappear. She went to stand beside Alan, who was flirting with Angela's sister, Sadie.

'You OK?' he said. 'You look a little alarmed.'

'It's not really going according to plan,' she whispered to him. But Alan, like everyone else, was staring at the piano as Reggie had started playing and Alice was standing beside him with her hands on her hips and a toothy smile on her face.

'*When the moon hits your eye like a big pizza pie…*' Alice began, and the guests yelled out encouragement. Alice's voice hadn't improved but she was confident, and she moved around the delighted guests urging them to join in, comfortable as the centre of attention, using tricks she'd picked up on the cruise ship to dodge the groping hands of old men and get everyone, even the waiters, joining in. Some sang along, some swayed, all of them smiled at her. Natalie started laughing. It was great. As Alice ended the song, and Reggie performed a glissando on the piano, she found herself joining the crowd in yelling for more.

IV

When it gets cold in New York, eyelashes freeze, it's hard to breathe and most people stay indoors. Natalie had a route to work that kept her mostly underground. There was a short but difficult walk to the subway, a crowded, smelly ride and then she'd come up for air right in front of the office building where she'd been working for six months. Her British university degree didn't open doors as she'd expected, so she'd taken a job as a secretary to the managing director of an ad agency. She didn't have a lot to do, but he loved her English accent and liked her to interrupt meetings now and again to show her off to his peers. Natalie would come into the board room to hand over requested papers which he didn't look at, instead asking her a series of questions so that she could display her Mary Poppins' voice and manners. She started dressing in more formal suits and the occasional pussy-bow shirt, figuring if that's what she was being paid for, she'd deliver to the best of her ability.

Her boss had a reputation for being difficult, but he never yelled at Natalie. He saw her as part of his brand, a status symbol, and even apologized if anyone swore in front of her. The other girls said Natalie could get away with anything, but she didn't take advantage. Although she was grateful when she had to take a few days off to take Sal to rehab and her boss said she didn't have to take it as vacation.

It had taken months of research, persuasion and false starts to get Sal into rehab. They'd got into a routine pretty quickly after the wedding, with him being fun and helpful throughout the week and each weekend being a mess. Mondays always started with an apology and a promise that he'd get himself together. There was always some reason for why he had needed to 'let off steam' which he'd beg her to understand, followed by a declaration of his love for her and a solemn vow, made through tears, that he'd never get that bad again. Natalie was out of her depth. Sometimes she tried to join him taking coke, but she hated how she couldn't think straight for days after and she realised that he preferred to be alone when he was high anyway. The times they had together could be fun and playful; he bought her presents, agreed to the transformation of their Brooklyn home, made her feel that she was the only woman who'd ever understood him. It was confusing and for the first few months at least she ignored his addiction as he had. She didn't really want to deal with it. Also, it was the best 'get out of jail free' card you could ever wish for. Whatever she did, whether coming home late, leaving the kitchen a mess or ignoring his friends at parties, it could never be as bad as what he was doing. She was good and he was bad. This was reinforced by members of Sal's family who openly called her 'his saviour' and their friends who would occasionally take her to one side and marvel at how Sal had managed to get her as a wife. She didn't allow herself to think along those lines, even when Sal, in a rage, pushed her against the wall and held his hand against her neck threatening to finish her off if she didn't leave him alone to live his life as he wanted.

Within six months the weekends and the weekdays were interchangeable. Sal went into work only when he felt like it and was getting more secretive about what he was doing. Natalie dealt with him carefully, recognizing that there was a certain point, just before the excitement kicked in of his next binge and certainly a long time after his last come down, that she could talk about anything serious with him.

They'd spoken about a residential rehab, even received a couple of brochures through the mail, but he had many arguments for why this wouldn't work. Then one day he changed his mind. One morning, she woke up to Sal not sitting on the couch sweating out the night's cocaine but flicking through the brochures. Natalie wanted to ask him what had brought about this change, but she thought wiser of it. Instead, she helped him pack a bag, oversaw the arrangements for his check-in and drove him up to Syracuse to drop him off.

When Angela suggested they take Grandma out for lunch, Natalie wondered how she was going to explain Sal's trip upstate. She needn't have worried. Angela knew, and she patted Natalie's arm and told her that she'd done the right thing.

'Well, it was Sal's decision,' Natalie said, but Angela wasn't listening.

They were in a restaurant that wasn't anywhere near as nice as the nursing home where Grandma took most of her meals, but Grandma said she preferred it. She was in good spirits and enjoying herself. They wheeled her to a table by the window and ordered baked clams. The three women discussed the usual topics: the food and how the sauce might be achieved, Natalie's work and how impressed they were that she was working in Manhattan because office life beat working in a shop, and how the old lady's various ailments were causing the doctors a hell of a time with their prescriptions.

'My momma lived until she was hundred,' Grandma said. 'But she had the devil on her side.'

'She wasn't 100,' whispered Angela to Natalie.

After dinner and a good conversation with the waiter about the how the chef managed to get the dessert so creamy, they left. Natalie helped Angela manoeuvre Grandma into the car and fold up the wheelchair.

'I need to talk to you alone, sweetie,' said Angela, closing the car door and leaving Grandma to watch through the window.

'Everything ok?' asked Natalie.

'Seems that Sal has done something to get us all in trouble this time.' She took a moment to mutter something in Italian under her breath. Grandma watched them both closely. 'He's made a mistake and it's going to cost me and Grandma. They're going to stop paying,' she started to cry a little, 'because of what that stupid guy did.'

'Oh, God, surely there's something I can do?' Natalie touched Angela's arm.

'It's do with Felicity, the goomah. He took something from her when he went around to her house.'

Natalie knew who Angela referred to. Felicity was the long-time girlfriend of Sal's married boss, Grandma's benefactor. Natalie had even met her once when she'd picked Sal up from her condominium after he'd been there to set up her computer. In her late 50s, the small round woman had come to the door in a housecoat patterned with big orange flowers and an orange hairpiece to match. She'd insisted that Natalie stay for some food and wouldn't take no for an answer. Natalie decided she'd try and talk to her; maybe in some way this could be worked out.

Felicity's condominium was in a tall building with balconies that looked over the Long Island Expressway and beyond to Jamaica and the airport. Natalie pressed the buzzer for Felicity before she'd really worked out what she was going to say.

'Who's that?' came a response and Natalie recognized Felicity's voice.

'It's Natalie, Sal's wife,' she stumbled with her words.

'What do you want?'

'I just thought I might come and have a chat; it seems there's been a bit of a problem... '

'You're not getting any money out of me.' Felicity's voice was cold.

'No, no, I don't want money, just want to talk to you, I thought perhaps if I could just explain... '

The buzzer unlatched the door, and Natalie entered. When the elevator doors opened on the top floor, she could see Felicity standing in the doorway to her apartment.

'I remember you, English,' Felicity said as Natalie approached.

'Thanks so much for seeing me, Mrs... Miss...' Natalie held out her hand. 'I'm Natalie.'

Felicity opened the door wider. 'Come on in, but I warn ya, I ain't in a great mood.'

Felicity's open plan apartment was an interior decorator's experiment in colour co-ordination. The pale blue of the walls was picked up exactly in the piping along the sofa cushions; the silver of the lamps matched the tin-toned curtains, and the thick carpet incorporated both colours in a giant fleur-de-lis pattern that was echoed on the kitchen cabinets.

Felicity invited her to sit down and went to get her coffee from the kitchen area.

'Perhaps I can start by saying, I don't know exactly what Sal's done but I'm here to see if I can help put it right.'

Felicity smirked as Natalie rambled on.

'I know you don't know me very well, but I can assure you that I'm completely happy to do whatever it takes to fix the problem that Sal's gotten himself into.'

Felicity blew on her coffee, although it didn't look hot, and leaned on the dining table. 'Your son of a bitch husband stole from me and instead of owning up he's just taken himself out of the picture.'

'He's in rehab. It's impossible to contact him at the moment. I know that's bad timing.'

'As soon as the heat is on him, he checks himself in? He knows the guys were looking for him.'

'He's got a drug problem, he's trying to get on top of it.'

Felicity stared at the young woman sitting on her sofa with a look of amused pity. Her voice softened. 'He's in some serious trouble, honey. This isn't something you can help him with. You see, what he did… ' Felicity stood and moved over to Natalie, tucking herself into the sofa seat beside her so their legs touched '… what he did, embarrassed me. It's kind of a thing with me and my guy. We hate to be embarrassed.'

'Oh, I completely understand. There's nothing worse.' Natalie was trembling a little.

'You seem like a nice girl; take some advice from me, will ya?'

Natalie nodded.

'Get the fuck out of there. Junkies never change. Run if you can, before he takes you down with him.'

'He's going to have to…'

'He's going to do fuck all, for ever. That's how it works. I know what I'm talking about, English.'

Natalie was really shaking now, and Felicity got her a drink, handing over a little glass of aquavit that stung as she swallowed it.

'Calm yourself down,' said Felicity. 'You take a moment now and calm yourself down. You're going to have enough to deal with, with the baby and all.'

'I'm not pregnant,' said Natalie.

'Yeah, you are.' When Natalie shook her head, Felicity reached to touch her stomach. 'I got a feeling for these things.'

Once Natalie had settled enough to breathe properly, she thanked Felicity for her time and got up to leave.

'I appreciate you coming though, English', Felicity went to open the door. 'You're gutsy. I'll give you that. It's not going to change things with Sal, but you can tell Angela and Josepina not to worry, OK?'

'Thanks, thanks so much.'

The elevator took a while to arrive at the top floor and, with Felicity back inside her apartment, Natalie stood on her own looking at her reflection in the shiny doors. She had wanted to give up saving people. She had thought that leaving London and marrying this older guy would be the end of all that. Sometimes it seemed to Natalie, that ever since she'd been plucked from the sea as a kid, she'd spent all her time paying that back, pulling everyone else to safety. She was exhausted. The elevator arrived with a loud 'bing'. Natalie just wanted to go home, get into bed and sleep for a month.

In Sal's absence, Natalie made changes to the apartment and it now had a welcoming style, as English as American, with a bookcase of paperbacks, a framed poster from The Met Opera and embroidered cushions on each sofa and chair. She had a photo from her wedding day that should have been on display, but she hadn't put it in a frame yet. This photo of them in their finery remained in the envelope it had been delivered in, in a drawer in the bedroom. The dog now slept indoors and had transformed from a rather twitchy guard dog into a lazy affectionate pup, who laid her head on Natalie's lap as she watched TV and took up the bottom half of her bed each night. Natalie had broken the rehab rules about no contact to get a message to Sal that she was pregnant. She hadn't heard back from him yet and wasn't sure how that was all going to work out. With him away for a while, she seemed to have so much time on her hands and was feeling positive for a change. Natalie worked for the ad agency during the week. She'd been given the job of arranging a client party and was pulling together an event with millimetre precision, creating a bit of theatre that even her father would have appreciated. She'd take the dog for long walks at the weekend and spend the afternoons reading baby books. She'd also called her mother in London to give her the news about her pregnancy. She'd spoken with Alice who was back at the flat and said she'd pass on the message.

One day she picked up Grandma from the nursing home and drove her to the apartment so that they could spend time cooking together. The old lady's wheelchair was positioned in the corner of the small kitchen as Natalie prepared ingredients according to her instructions. They were making pasta, without a machine, using a knife to draw lines in the dough and placing mounds of sauce in rows to fill little pillows of ravioli.

'Your momma cook?' Grandma's face was at chin-level to the floury counter-top.

'Not like this,' said Natalie. 'She does a great Sunday lunch though.'

'You show me one day. You miss your momma?' Grandma reached over to pinch the already pinched ravioli, fixing Natalie's clumsy effort.

'Yes, I do. I hope we can work things out between us before the baby comes.'

'My first baby had golden hair and blue eyes. Little Maria was an angel from Jesus.'

'I bet she was beautiful.'

Grandma huffed. She pointed to her handbag that was hanging over the back of her wheelchair. Natalie retrieved it for her. Grandma fumbled around for a moment and then pulled out a little sliver of red ribbon. She held it up and spat on it. Natalie watched her closely. She'd spent enough time with the old lady now to know not to question her unusual habits.

'Pin this on your clothes,' she said. 'You have to be very very careful. People do bad things. Some want evil.'

Natalie humoured her grandmother-in-law by fetching a safety pin and fixing the ribbon onto her T-shirt.

'Babies are from heaven and you have to keep your eye open – always eye open.'

'I will, I promise. '

'A little baby has a light in it, coming from it. It draws in... you know.'

'I think I know what you mean. My mum's friend, Bobbi, said similar things. She said that humans gave off a light, like a firefly.'

'She knows. Now put on a big pan of water.'

Natalie struggled to fill the giant pan and carried it towards the counter. 'Is this for the baby too?'

'For the ravioli,' the old lady laughed. She reached out and smacked Natalie on the leg.

Once the pasta was ready, Natalie served it in two dishes with some olive oil and the two women sat silently to eat it. Natalie smiled at Grandma and the old lady winked at her.

'If I ever get my Mum to come and visit me, I'll cook this for her,' Natalie said.

'She'll come. The baby will draw her in. My mother, oh no.' Grandma paused for effect. 'She hated me. Angry all the time. Hated the babies.' Grandma was laughing now. 'She miserable, miserable jealous woman. She was in love with my husband.'

'Really? Well, I don't think I have that problem with my Mum.'

'That summa bitch Sal. He's like my Sal. No good from that man.'

'Oh, Grandma, he's trying to change.'

'Don't you care any more, don't worry about him. You will have your baby and she will make you happy. No man made me happy.'

'You think I'll have a daughter?'

'I had three girls. Three little angels from Jesus. But they grow, they're ungrateful. I say, you get the baby for you. Don't expect them to say thank you. The men, pppfff, they come sometimes, they go sometimes. The baby is for you. You hear me?'

Natalie got up to clear away the plates and seeing that Grandma's eyes were drooping, she wheeled her into the bedroom and helped her onto the bed for a nap, kicking the dog out of the room before closing the door as the old lady started to snore.

Natalie looked at her own reflection in the hallway mirror and touched at the red ribbon on her shirt. She'd make sure she'd wear it whenever she saw Grandma. Although she was too practical a person to believe in her superstitions, Natalie was charmed by the old lady's stories. Maybe one day she should write them down. Despite being pregnant and knowing at some point she'd have to deal with Sal, Natalie felt calm, happy in a way. She could do this. She had her job for money and Angela had promised to help look after the baby. Natalie's eyes twinkled, and she realised how pretty she looked in the mirror. Just to be on the safe side, she did a dry spit on the floor and smiled at her own foolishness.

Then phone rang, and it was her mother.

V

Veronica and Alexander sat upright at a table on the street outside a Greenwich Village venue, looking uncomfortable. Natalie could see them as soon as she turned the block. Other

New Yorkers lounged and chatted around them and the waitress brought over two cups of coffee and a slice of cake. They hadn't spotted her yet and she watched them for a moment. Her brother was a man now. He had long straggly hair, arms that stretched the sleeves of his T-shirt and he was smoking. Natalie smiled. Veronica must have mellowed a bit. Natalie would never have dared light a cigarette in front of her when she was Alex's age.

As Natalie dodged the people meandering down the street, her mother and brother spotted her. They both stood. She noticed her mother looking a little panicked for a second before a broad, well-rehearsed smile stretched across her face. Natalie went forward and hugged her first. It seemed like the right thing to do. Veronica held the hug longer than Natalie was expecting, then looked down at her daughter's belly.

'A baby,' Veronica said. 'My first grandchild. It's so exciting. How are you feeling?'

And that was enough. They chatted; they ordered more coffee when theirs was finished; they spoke over each other, interrupting and carrying on multiple conversations in the way their family always had, a way that kept outsiders confused but they found energising and familiar. Without mentioning anything that had happened or the twelve months it had been since they'd last spoken, Natalie was back in the family.

Natalie told them about her job and how she was going to change it soon. Once the baby was born, she'd start looking for something that suited her better. Alex recounted stories about his gap year and said that he wanted to go to film school and was checking out NYU even though the costs were exorbitant, and Alan had said he couldn't afford any more school fees.

'You get a grant if you study in England,' said Veronica.

'Yeah, I know. I'm only looking.' Alex reached to light another cigarette.

'Must you?' Veronica shook her head at him. 'I'm singing tonight and I'd rather you didn't.'

'You've got a gig?' Natalie asked.

'Reggie's got me on here. I've got you a couple of tickets, if you'd like to come.'

'I'd love to. I'll come on my own, though. Sal's away.'

They stayed chatting until it got too chilly to sit outside. Then the siblings went to the bar for a drink while their mother disappeared to get changed and warm up. Reggie arrived for the evening's entertainment and came over to say hello.

'All going well?' he asked.

'Thanks, Reggie,' said Natalie. 'It feels so good to see her again.'

When Reggie had vanished through to the stage area, Alex raised his glass to his sister.

'Happy families,' he said. They clinked glasses.

'Thank fuck for that,' said Natalie. 'Do you ever think we'll discuss what happened? Will she apologise for cutting me off like that? Or forgive me for leaving her high and dry?'

Alex laughed. 'Don't push it. This is how it is, Natalie. You know that. That was how things were and this is how things are now. New show, new part to play, curtain up.'

'I wonder if she's looking forward to playing a grandmother?'

Alex laughed again and drained his glass. 'Come on, let's get seated.'

The siblings found a table near the front. Natalie took off her coat and fixed the little red ribbon that she was now wearing every day.

'What's that?' Alex asked as he noticed his sister fiddling with the frayed material.

'A little bit of Sicilian magic. I got it from Sal's grandmother. You'll love her. Perhaps I can take you to meet her while you're here. She's incredible. And his mother's lovely too. I can't wait for you to meet them.'

'And Sal?'

'That's another conversation. All the magic in the world might not fix him.'

The lights dimmed, and Reggie came on stage to applause and shouts from the noisy crowd. He played for a while, and the crowd chatted as the room filled up.

By the time Reggie introduced Veronica, the room was packed. Natalie and Alex were sharing their table and people were standing behind and beside them. Veronica held her head high as she stepped up on the stage, looking over to her two children and blowing them a kiss. She moved just below the spotlight, which beamed down onto the darkened stage, catching the tiny flecks of dust that shimmered as if in water. Veronica's red hair, cropped into a pixie cut, picked up the light and glowed. Her eyes sparkled.

'I put a spell on you ...'

Reggie began stroking the keys of the piano and the two of them filled the room with beautiful sound. Veronica's voice had the same mesmerising quality that it always had had, drawing in the audience so that they smiled and looked to one another to confirm that they were witnessing something extraordinary. It was Veronica's unique talent; it had never left her. It was a warm stream of familiarity that reached deep into Natalie, reminding her of every lullaby, every show she'd seen her mother in, every recording she'd made and played on their little turntable, wherever they'd been living, whatever crisis they'd been dealing with, whoever was in their life or missing. Natalie put her hand on her own round tummy and wondered if her baby could hear. She felt inspired. Natalie would find her own undeniable gift soon enough, whatever that was.

'That your Mom?' a guy sharing her table leaned over and asked. Natalie smiled at him.

'I put a spell on you ... because you're mine.'